THE GOLDEN SPANIARD

Kristie knew that Manuel Montevio was not keen on being interviewed, but she had not realised the lengths to which he was prepared to go to keep journalists like herself at a distance—until it was too late!

Books you will enjoy
by REBECCA STRATTON

DARK ENIGMA

After four years looking after little orphaned Niki, Carey was taking him to Greece to live with his mother's family. She wasn't at all happy about leaving the child with his uncle, the stern and enigmatic Dimitri Karamalis, and she was even more concerned that Niki would still not have a mother. But what could she do about it?

THE BLACK INVADER

It wasn't Miguel Montañas' fault that his family now owned the home that had meant so much to Kirstie for so long—but illogically she blamed him for everything. More than one person had hinted that one solution to her problem would be for her and Miguel to marry—but why should she, even in the unlikely event of his asking her?

THE SILKEN CAGE

Worried to death about what had become of her twin brother Peter, Troy went off to Morocco to look for him. And discovered, to her cost, that the one man who might have been able to help her, the impressive and powerful Kadir ben Raschid, was the man who also wanted to find Peter—to be revenged on him!

THE INHERITED BRIDE

'I'd marry the devil's daughter to get Anchoterrias,' declared Eduardo Sagrera—but in fact he married Lari, who had inherited the property herself. Even though—at first, at any rate—it was nothing but a marriage of convenience, Lari soon knew she wanted it to be much more. But the spiteful Juana Cortez was at hand to see that it wasn't!

THE GOLDEN SPANIARD

BY

REBECCA STRATTON

MILLS & BOON LIMITED
15-16 BROOK'S MEWS
LONDON W1A 1DR

First published 1982
Australian copyright 1982
Philippine copyright 1982
This edition 1982

© Rebecca Stratton 1982

ISBN 0 263 73748 9

Set in Monophoto Baskerville 10 on 10½ pt.

Made and printed in Great Britain by
Richard Clay (The Chaucer Press) Ltd,
Bungay, Suffolk

CHAPTER ONE

KRISTIE was beginning to have doubts, and that annoyed her, because her mind was firmly made up and she had no intention of changing it. She was also wishing she had come alone, but Juan had insisted on driving her, and Juan's brand of driving was not the kind to settle anyone's nerves. Kristie had long since noted a certain air of fatalism about any Spaniard when he was seated behind the wheel of a motor vehicle, and Juan Murillo was no exception.

He drove as if whatever was around the next bend would either get out of his way or not, it was in the hands of the Almighty if an accident happened. But he meant well, and Kristie had to admit that he gave a boost to her slightly wavering courage, so she took her mind off possible accidents by looking out of the window.

Seville at the height of summer was the hottest place in all Spain, and at least the speed of the car did something to relieve the oppressiveness by creating a breeze that blew in through the open windows. She looked out at the wide streets and *plazas* that were shaded by orange trees yet seemed to shimmer in the heat with a bright, bold picture-postcard look that she adored.

Kristie was familiar with Seville from numerous visits and she always revelled in the beauty of the ancient city, whose older houses with their iron-barred windows and cool *patios* suggested another, more gracious age. It gave her a sense of pride too, for her father had been born and raised there. Her father had been Spanish and she supposed that the feeling she had for the city of his birth was bred in her; a feeling that encompassed the whole of the hot and exotic Andalucian countryside.

José Roderigo had died in England nearly thirteen years ago, when his daughter was only ten years old, but he had any number of cousins in Spain who were ready and willing to see Kristie whenever she chose to visit them, and since she loved Spain so much she spent a holiday with one or another of them each year. Her present companion was the son of one of her father's cousins, and he and his widowed mother had welcomed her as warmly as all her Spanish relations did.

Aunt Maria, as Kristie called her, was not altogether happy about her son's free and easy association with his second cousin. But the formality of a chaperone had long since been abandoned in the bigger cities and towns, even though the tradition still lingered in the more remote country districts. Kristie's profession probably made her aunt vaguely uneasy too, for female newspaper reporters were something outside her experience.

It was because of something she had learned quite innocently in the course of a conversation with one of Juan's friends that Kristie was now driving out to a district on the more remote outskirts of Seville in search of a particular man. A man she knew only by repute and by way of her paper's archives.

Manuel Montevio, known as the Golden Spaniard, who only a few short years ago had been constantly in the headlines on the sporting pages. Haughty, enigmatic, intriguing; all those had been applied to Manuel Montevio during his fabulously successful career, as well as other, less flattering, terms that stemmed from his determined aloofness.

As a crack Grand Prix driver he had been news, then quite suddenly and dramatically, three years ago, he had dropped out of the public eye leaving a speculating press and public wondering at the reason for it. The speculation went on for weeks, and rumour ran riot for a while, but the former idol seemed to have completely disappeared, and fame being the fickle glory it is, interest eventually began to wane.

Sheer chance had put Kristie on the scent; a remark casually made during a friendly conversation but much too intriguing to be ignored by an ambitious young journalist anxious to make her way. 'I can still hardly believe 'my luck,' Kristie said, and the young man beside her and driving the car gave her a brief and faintly resigned glance from the corner of his eye.

'You're convinced Marcos was right,' he observed, 'I just hope you're not going to be disappointed, Kristie. He only caught a glimpse of him as he was leaving, remember, and the agent who interviewed him for the job saw him on behalf of a Señor Hernandez.'

'Well, he'd hardly use his own name if he wants to remain incognito,' Kristie insisted, 'and he's too well known for anyone to make a mistake about who he is. There aren't many men in Spain who look like him, and Marcos was a fan of his, he said, didn't he? No—if Marcos says Montevio is at the Villa de los Naranjos, then I believe him; after all, the man has to be *somewhere*.'

Juan shrugged. 'If you believe it,' he said.

In fact Kristie was so confident that their friend had made a right identification that she had lost no time in ringing her editor in London. Like Juan he had not been entirely convinced she wasn't chasing shadows, but since she was prepared to follow up the story in what was officially her holiday he wasn't averse to giving her the go-ahead.

Kristie for her part had confidently promised to come up with an interview with the elusive Golden Spaniard, and with the reason for his sudden and unexplained withdrawal from the limelight. The prospect thrilled and delighted her, for she had never had such an opportunity to prove herself before and she meant to make the most of it.

Even allowing that her information had been right, she didn't anticipate it would be easy, for the man in question had never had any liking for the press, in fact he had always gone out of his way to avoid reporters, and refused to give interviews. Kristie chose to ignore that side of his reputation, however, and looked upon this drive out to the Villa de los Naranjos as the first step in the biggest break of her career.

'You know that you're a mad, crazy Englishwoman?'

Juan said, and she gave him a half-smile.

'If you say so.'

His seemingly lighthearted words she knew concealed a very genuine concern that she was taking on more than she could cope with, and she appreciated it rather more than she let him know. 'You know, you won't get near him either, Kristie. Pretty as you are, he isn't going to make an exception of you; why should he?'

'Why should he?' Kristie echoed, and hoped her wavering confidence wasn't too obvious, for Juan needed very little encouragement to turn around and drive back home. 'There's an old English saying, Juan—nothing ventured, nothing gained, and it's very true. If I don't *try* to see him I'll never know whether he would have made me the exception or not, will I?'

Juan shrugged. Like most of his countrymen he found it a useful way of turning aside questions he would rather not answer, but he wouldn't give up trying to talk her out of it, Kristie knew. Juan had the same stubborn streak that she remembered in her father and, if she was honest enough to admit it, she possessed herself.

He was good-looking in what was generally considered to be a typically Spanish way; in fact he was a typical Andaluz, as her father had been. Medium tall and slim, he had black hair and dark, expressive eyes, and he never made any attempt to hide his admiration of her. His manners were impeccable always, but when he was alone with her he was sometimes inclined to adopt a slightly less formal manner in an attempt to match her Englishness.

'And why must you wear that awful wig?' he wanted to know.

The wig in question was very blonde and shiny and very unnatural, but it completely covered her own black hair and made her look entirely different from her normal self. Patting it in place a little selfconsciously, Kristie shrugged. 'It isn't awful,' she said defensively, and Juan gave a snort of laughter.

'It's hideous!' he declared. 'And I don't see the object of disguising yourself, Kristie; if you *are* going to have any success it won't be as a brassy blonde. Speaking from the man's point of view, you'd stand a much better chance as your own lovely self, my pigeon.'

He paid the compliment naturally and as a matter of course, as he always did, and Kristie smiled. In fact she wasn't quite sure why she'd elected to wear the wig; it had been a spur-of-the-moment thing, inspired, she supposed, by the somewhat dramatic and intriguing nature of the task she had set herself. Also, she realised, it made her feel slightly less vulnerable, although she disliked admitting it, even to herself.

'Manuel Montevio is notorious for his dislike of the press,' she reminded him, 'and it might help to keep a low profile initially. The wig at least gives the false impression that I'm blonde.'

'It does absolutely nothing for you,' Juan informed her bluntly. 'And it's wicked to disguise looks like yours in any way at all, and especially with that—that monstrosity.'

'Well, I feel better wearing it for the moment.'

Juan gave her a knowing look from the corner of his eye. 'You're getting scared,' he guessed, and his obvious satisfaction aroused her stubborn streak as nothing else could have done.

'I'd say I'm—wary!' she retorted. 'I'd be a fool not to feel a bit edgy in the circumstances, although I don't quite see what can go wrong. This is really no more than a recce—a chance to spy out the land and get some idea of the layout of the place.'

'Are you serious?' Juan asked, looking faintly shocked. 'I had no idea that journalism involved disguises and—spying out the land.'

'Well, now you do!' Kristie told him with a trace of irritation. 'I don't want to go in there blindly, knowing nothing about the place, or how hard it will be to get in. There might be guard dogs or——'

'Holy Mother!' Juan stared at her. 'Kristie, little pigeon, are you sure you wouldn't like to have second thoughts about this?'

'I'm quite sure,' Kristie assured him, and Juan shook his head at her despairingly.

At twenty-three she had the soft and vulnerable look of a girl several years younger, and it was hard to convince Juan that she did not need protecting. Her hair was as black as her father's had been, but she had the blue eyes and fair complexion of her mother, and the Spanish sun had barely touched the paleness of her cheeks as yet. Her mouth was softly full and it curved into a smile as she glanced sideways at Juan's frowning face.

'I just wish I knew more about the wretched man,' she said, hoping to turn his attention to the object of her interest instead. 'For someone who was so much in the public eye he was a bit of a mystery. He never gave interviews, so no one ever found out anything about his private life, or even his love life—if he had one.'

'And you hope to succeed where everyone else failed,' Juan guessed, though he obviously didn't anticipate her having much success, from the tone of his voice, and Kristie glanced at him briefly.

'I might just do that,' she said, and again looked at him curiously. 'Don't you approve, Juan? If you have a conscience about it just say so and I'll do it on my own; you can back out any time.'

He spared her a brief speculative glance as they sped through the hot green countryside. 'Do you want me to?'

Impulsively, as she did so many things, Kristie clasped her hands over his arm and hugged him for a second. 'It's rather nice having you around in case of emergencies,' she told him, and he smiled wryly.

'As it was through me that you found out about Manuel Montevio being in Seville,' he said, 'it's the least I can do. If Marcos Francisco hadn't mentioned that he was to be temporary secretary to him for three weeks you'd never have known Montevio was here, and I don't know whether to be pleased or sorry that you *do* know!'

'I'm pleased,' Kristie declared unhesitatingly. 'My stock with the editor will soar sky-high if I bring this off and it could lead to bigger and better assignments. Just imagine—no one has been able to trace him all this time and quite by chance one of your friends gets a job as his temporary secretary. Manuel Montevio—the Golden Spaniard; it's almost too much to believe!'

'You mean to be a successful career woman, don't you, Kristie?' Juan kept his eyes on the road, but something in his voice made Kristie turn and look at him, frowning slightly.

'That's the idea,' she agreed quietly, 'and I've done pretty well so far.'

'Interviewing ageing actresses, greedy for publicity, and housewives who have witnessed a local shop being robbed,' Juan said, reducing her achievements to the level of small-town gossip. 'That isn't big-time, Kristie, this is!'

She flushed, resenting the truth of what he said as much as the fact that he had been so cruelly honest. She knew perfectly well that if she did pull off this interview with Manuel Montevio it would the biggest thing she had done so far, but the nagging fear fluttered in her stomach that she might fail.

'And you think I'm not capable of handling it?' she demanded.

Juan looked much more serious and he did not automatically reassure her as she wished him to. Instead he was shaking his head slowly and the brief glance he sent her suggested anxiety as well as regret. 'I can't help thinking,' he said, 'that your father wouldn't have approved of what you're doing—or proposing to do.'

'I'm doing my job,' Kristie insisted, hating to admit that he was probably right about her father. 'And you don't have the right to criticise me for doing it to the best of my ability, Juan—you're not my keeper!'

'I'm sorry!'

His good-looking face had a tight closed look suddenly, and she realised how close they came to quarrelling. It was the very last thing she wanted, for she was very fond of Juan, and she appreciated his willingness to go along with her on what might well prove to be a wild-goose chase, even though she suspected he indulged her against his better judgment.

Juan was modern enough in his outlook most of the time, but there were occasions when he could be as strongly traditional as his mother. He left her no doubt that he felt she needed protection from the harsher realities of the world, and she felt flattered but at the same time vaguely irritated by it. Placing a hand on his arm, she closed her fingers over the tenseness of the muscles under his shirt sleeve and smiled up at him tentatively.

'I'm sorry, Juan,' she said softly. 'I didn't mean to sound so ungrateful.'

Swiftly a glowing dark gaze swept over her face and came to rest briefly on her mouth. 'You don't have to be grateful,' he said. 'And I didn't really mean to sound like a disapproving parent; I just can't get used to the idea of you as a hardboiled press woman, Kristie. You were fifteen the last time you stayed with us, and you don't look very much older now.'

'Eight years,' Kristie reminded him, then grasped his arm more tightly suddenly when a *patio*-surrounded house appeared in front of them around the next bend.

Unless they had been misdirected this must be the Villa de los Naranjos, and her heart was racing hard as she watched glimpses of red roof flutter in and out of the treetops that surrounded it. She told herself that it was sheer excitement that caused her heart to race as it did, but deep down she recognised apprehension too. She would never admit that tackling Manuel Montevio was beyond her, but she should surely not have felt so dismayingly sick as Juan turned into a short narrow access road that led only to a low arched gateway, shaded by the orange trees that gave the villa its name.

The house itself was barely visible behind the lush gardens that overflowed on to the *patio* paths, but its series of red-tiled roofs on various levels gave an indication of its size, and to Kristie it looked huge. There were glimpses of balconies draped with red roses and garlands of bougainvillea, and cool arched windows set back under sweeping eaves that gave shade from the searching heat of the sun.

Directly facing them as they sat in the car was an enormous wrought iron gate that was very pointedly padlocked against intruders, and immediately beyond it a large garage that must have been capable of housing at least three cars. Just briefly her spirit almost yielded before the enormity of the task she had set herself, but the thought of what it could mean to her career if she succeeded stopped her from weakening.

By fair means or foul she meant to get past that padlocked gate and talk with the man who so determinedly kept the world at arm's length, but how? After several moments staring at the gate in gloomy silence, Kristie turned and looked at Juan, putting a hand on his arm and pressing lightly with her fingertips.

'Go and see what you can see, Juan,' she asked, and he looked at her doubtfully.

'There's nothing to see except an empty *patio* and a garage.' He heaved a deep sigh of resignation suddenly and turned in his seat. 'O.K., O.K., I'll go and see what I can see, although I wish I knew what I was looking for.'

'Anything,' Kristie told him. 'Warning systems, dogs, anything that looks as if it's there to prevent people approaching the house in the ordinary way.'

'And suppose someone comes along and takes me for a hopeful burglar?'

'Of course they won't, you look much too respectable! If someone *does* come say—well, anything. After all, you're not on the property, so you can't be chased off.'

Sighing deeply, Juan got out of the car, and with obvious reluctance walked across to the locked gate. Apparently because he could think of nothing better to do he gripped the ornate scrollwork and gave it an experimental shake before peering through at the gardens. It was almost as if he came in response to the rattle of the gate when an elderly man appeared as if by magic from behind the scented mass of a huge magnolia, and Juan started visibly, taking an involuntary step back.

'*Señor?*'

The enquiry was polite, but sharp old eyes took stock of him before shifting across to where Kristie sat in the passenger seat of the car. He couldn't have seen her very well, but she instinctively shrank back, although Juan was in full view and easily identifiable. It was impossible to guess what prompted him to act as he did, but Kristie could only attribute it to panic.

'I wonder if it's possible for this young lady to speak to Señor Hernandez,' he said, indicating her with a vague wave of his hand. 'It's about—business.'

The old man frowned suspiciously, and in the circumstances Kristie could hardly blame him as she sat staring in dismay at him. 'The *señor* sees no one,' the man declared firmly.

'Then is it possible to make an appointment?' Juan plunged on recklessly, and Kristie groaning inwardly, waiting for the reply.

'I think not, *señor*.'

'It's rather important,' Juan urged, and Kristie called out to him in desperation:

'Juan, please leave it! Please—don't say any more, leave it!'

He turned for a moment and looked at her in vague surprise, then turned again to the old man, who had murmured something Kristie was unable to catch. She saw Juan shrug and spread his hands, then as he turned and came back to the car the old man went trudging back through the gardens, still muttering to himself.

'What on earth made you ask for an appointment?' Kristie demanded when Juan came and leaned on the car beside her instead of getting back in, and he looked faintly disgruntled because she sounded so short with him.

'I thought you wanted to see the man,' he said, resting one arm on the roof. 'I was trying to help.' Bending his head, he peered in at her and she saw a glimmer of laughter in his eyes. 'Mind you, I don't think it will work, because according to the old fellow all foreign ladies are crazy, and apparently you're no exception.'

'Foreign?' Kristie echoed indignantly. 'Did you tell him I was foreign?'

Juan shook his head. 'I didn't have to, Kristie. You still have a very slight accent, you know, and it gets more pronounced when you're agitated.'

Kristie's blue eyes gleamed. So far the trip had proved nothing beyond the fact that the gate into the villa was not only padlocked but guarded, neither of which was encouraging. Quite frankly she could see no hope of gaining access in the normal way at the moment, and she sighed as she looked up at Juan standing beside her.

'We might as well go,' she told him. 'We can't do anything else today, although I think you've done quite enough already. The old man is sure to tell Montevio that there's been a foreign woman asking for an appointment with him and he'll be on his guard.'

Juan said nothing, but he looked both resentful and reproachful as he came and got back into the car. He was on the point of starting the engine when Kristie put a hand on his arm and pressed hard, and when he looked round at her and frowned, she nodded her head in the direction of the gate.

It had obviously been considered more convenient to have the garage built near to the gate and it stood on a small area of concrete that was screened from the *patio* by a hedge of shrubs. Kristie had noticed someone come through a break in the hedge from the direction of the house, and it took only a moment to recognise the newcomer for who he was.

'It's him!' she breathed, digging her fingers hard into Juan's arm. 'It's Montevio!'

'And he's coming to order us off,' Juan observed when the man changed direction suddenly and came along the short driveway to the gate. He looked angry and not in the least encouraging, but to Kristie this was an opportunity she hadn't dreamed she would have; having Manuel Montevio there in front of her. 'We'd better go, Kristie.'

'No, no, not yet!'

He stood immediately behind the gate and Kristie

fought down all kinds of panic and wild excitement as she sought desperately for an opening. 'You're parked on private property, *señor*,' he said, addressing Juan who sat as if transfixed behind the wheel. 'I'll be obliged if you'll move so that I can get my car out.'

Juan, she thought, would have obeyed instantly, deterred by the stern and vaguely menacing look fixed on him, but Kristie was already taking a hand. Leaning half out of the window, she called to him, her face flushed and the garishly blonde wig a little awry. '*Señor*,' she called, 'if you could spare me a minute——'

'I have no time to spare, *señora*, I am on my way to an appointment, if you will kindly get out of my way.'

He obviously assumed that she and Juan were husband and wife, but that didn't concern her at the moment, she was only anxious not to lose the chance that had dropped into her lap so unexpectedly. 'This wouldn't take a minute,' she insisted. 'If you'll just——'

'If you'll just move your car.' The firm voice had a touch of harshness that should have told her she had no chance at all. 'I've already said I have an appointment.'

'But——'

'Be so good as to move from my driveway, *señor*!'

He ignored her and again addressed himself to Juan, who was much more willing to do as he said, except that Kristie's hand on his arm restrained him. Her other hand was gripping the door as she leaned half out of the window, and it was doubtful if Manuel Montevio had a very good view of her from where he stood, except to note that she wore no wedding ring.

Her features were barely distinguishable, patterned as they were by the shifting patterns of leaves on the trees overhead, and also he was too far to one side to have a clear view of her around the edge of the windscreen, a situation that suited her at the moment while she felt her way. Her view of him on the other hand, was excellent, and she had to admit that what she saw was very impressive, even it was discouraging. Everything she saw confirmed her belief that she had done what no other press man or woman had succeeded in doing so far—she had tracked down the elusive Montevio.

Tall and arrogant, and with the lean ranginess of a cat, he also had the same suggestion of suppressed power. His hair was red-gold and grew thickly, like the lashes that shaded deep amber eyes, merging rather than contrasting with a teak brown complexion, so that the overall impression was one of rich, glowing gold. The Golden Spaniard.

He was impressive and disturbing in a way that was completely unexpected, so that Kristie found herself much more confused and uncertain than she ever remembered being before. He looked so physically powerful that she shivered, and there was an air of aloofness about him that confirmed his reputation. If this man chose not to reveal his private life to anyone he wouldn't allow himself to be harried into changing his mind, and yet she had committed herself to doing more or less that.

His dark grey suit was impeccably tailored and made the most of broad shoulders and lean hips, and a cream shirt showed a deep chest and a length of brown throat where a pulse beat steadily, but surely more heavily than normal. He was, Kristie concluded a little dazedly, much more attractive than she had been led to expect from old newspaper photographs.

'I presume you're the young woman who asked for an appointment to see me,' the quiet firm voice resumed. 'I thought my man had made it clear that I see no one, *señorita*. I dislike strangers arriving at my gate and making demands on my time, and I'll be obliged if you'll get your car out of the way so that I can drive out. *Adios!*'

He had turned and was walking back to the garage, presumably expecting no more opposition, and Kristie's reaction was purely automatic, her voice light and breathless. 'Señor Montevio!'

He stiffened, coming to a halt at once, then turned slowly and the amber eyes between their thick golden lashes gleamed angrily. 'You have decided to come into the open,' he said in a flat cold voice that sent a tremor of alarm through her, and Kristie saw herself with little option but to go on.

'I'm sorry I didn't approach you directly, *señor*,' she said in an incredibly shaky voice, 'but I didn't think you'd see me——'

'You assumed correctly, *señorita*!'

'I just want a few moments of your time, Señor Montevio, that's all.' She pressed on desperately, although she knew in her heart she was fighting a losing battle. 'If I could just speak with you——'

'You're a reporter, of course?' His expression suggested that she would have been more welcome had she brought the plague to his gate, and his eyes were fixed on her with such withering scorn that she curled up inside. 'I have no wish to speak to any member of the press, *señorita*, now or ever, and I never change my mind, so don't bother to come back!'

He turned and walked away with all the arrogance of a man dismissing someone he considered beneath his contempt, leaving Kristie staring after him in angry frustration. His back was as straight as a ramrod and the stiffness of anger was unmistakable in his stride as she sat and watched him open up the big garage doors, then she turned to Juan.

'Let's go,' she said in a brittle voice that echoed the brightness of anger in her eyes. 'He might just run us down, I wouldn't put it past him! Oh, damn it, Juan, why did it all have to go so wrong?'

For the moment Juan said nothing; he concentrated on backing the car out of the narrow access road, then gave her a brief glance from the corner of his eye. 'Can't you see it yet, Kristie? He isn't going to be persuaded, you heard what he said, and I believe him! More experienced people than you have tried and failed, so why not admit you simply can't do it?'

'Because I don't believe it!' She stared morosely at the road ahead, flushed with anger and bitter with disappointment, but she wouldn't admit defeat. 'Next time I'll be more cunning!'

'*Next* time?' Juan's dark eyes appealed to heaven.

'It's as well he didn't get a good look at me; he only saw a bit of my face and he'll be on the look-out for a blonde, so that will make it easier for me.'

'Kristie, why not give in gracefully? Please, *chica*!'

'Because I'm a journalist,' Kristie insisted stubbornly, and Juan heaved a great sigh of resignation.

'I give up!'

They were approaching the corner and he was obliged to manoeuvre hastily to avoid collision with a small van that came round at the same moment from the opposite direction. Kristie, however, was too involved with her own problems to take much notice, although she did vaguely register the fact that it had a familiar name on the side of it.

'I haven't finished with Señor Montevio by a long chalk!' she went on doggedly. 'I just need more time and preparation, that's all! Speaking to me as if I was the lowest form of life—I'll show him!'

It was two days since Kristie's chastening encounter with Manuel Montevio, and ever since she had been brooding on ways of getting to him, for she was as determined as ever to get an interview with him, one way or another. Having dismissed as unworkable the idea of appealing to his better nature by telling him how important it was to her career, she sought more devious ways, but so far ideas had been disappointingly few.

It was meeting by chance with a friend that gave her the nucleus of an idea, and while he and Juan talked together in the friendly clatter of their favourite café she worked out something that she thought had a fair chance of success.

Paco Armandaz's family owned a chain of grocery stores in and around Seville, and their small colourful vans were a familiar sight in the city streets as well as in the surrounding districts. Her aunt was a regular customer, but more to the point was Kristie's recollection of a near collision with one of the vans a couple of days ago when she and Juan were driving away from the Villa de los Naranjos.

Maybe the van hadn't been delivering to the villa, but there was every possibility it had been, and that was all the encouragement she needed. 'Paco, do you deliver to the Villa de los Naranjos on the San Pedro Road?'

Both turned to her and frowned. They had been discussing the latest performance of their favourite football team, and it was a moment before her question registered. 'Oh, you mean do we deliver groceries to them?' Paco said, when the light dawned. 'It's quite possible, Kristie, we deliver all over the place.' He cocked a dark eye at her curiously. 'Why?'

'Could you find out for certain?'

She was aware of Juan from the corner of her eye, frowning suspiciously at her, and she hoped he wasn't going to say something and spoil her idea. 'I could,' Paco told her, and glanced curiously at Juan. 'But what is all this? Do you know, *amigo*? Has your gorgeous cousin gone crazy?'

'I'd be grateful if you would find out for me,' said Kristie, speaking up quickly before Juan said anything. 'I'd just like to know if they have a regular weekly order, like Aunt Maria does.'

Paco was obviously puzzled as well as intrigued, and he again glanced at Juan, as if he hoped he would provide the answer. 'I'll find out by all means, if it's important to you, Kristie, although I can't imagine why it should be.'

'It's some wild scheme she's cooking up,' Juan guessed, and it was obvious he hoped to persuade Paco against helping her in any way at all. 'Kristie, please don't start anything we'll all live to regret.'

Kristie ran a fingertip around the rim of her wine glass, ignoring his advice and concentrating on enlightening Paco Armandaz as much as she safely could. 'You know I work for a newspaper, don't you, Paco?' He nodded, and the glance he gave Juan this time was slightly more wary. 'There's someone living at the Villa de los Naranjos that I want to interview,' she went on, 'and I need to get into the villa grounds at least.'

'But how can I help?'

Still she hesitated to go too fast for fear of frightening him off; and she knew exactly how Juan would react. 'You could prepare the way for me,' she told Paco, and putting her hands tightly together on the table in front of her she tried out her scheme verbally for the first time. 'My idea is to fit myself out with boy's clothes; trousers, shirt and a cap to hid my hair, then get into the villa grounds as a van-boy in one of your delivery vans when it takes the weekly order.'

'Holy Mother of God!' Juan breathed, and hid his face in his hands for a moment. 'You *are* crazy! You'd never get away with a scheme like that, Kristie, and if you did manage to get in you run the risk of being arrested for trespass, if not something worse!'

'We'll see,' Kristie insisted, and looked to Paco to support her. 'I can do it, Paco, if you'll help.'

Clearly some of Juan's caution had rubbed off, for Paco looked less encouraging, and yet he did not entirely dismiss the idea. 'I can find out if we deliver, of course,' he said.

'And arrange for the driver to take me in, if you do deliver?' Kristie urged. 'Please, Paco, this is really very important to me; so far I have an exclusive on this story, and if I can just get an interview before anyone else finds out where—Well, I won't say any more, except that I'll be eternally grateful to you if this comes off, as I hope it will.'

Paco smiled at her a little wryly, and just briefly his eyes strayed to the open neck of her dress. 'I hope it does,' he told her. 'But if you're seriously thinking of passing yourself off as a boy you'd better get a very loose-fitting shirt or you'll never get away with it.'

The fact that Kristie coloured as she did was due mainly to the fact that she was aware of just how much Juan would dislike the observation, and with that in mind she made light of it. 'Oh, don't worry about that,' she said, 'I'll make sure I pass. As long as I can depend on you doing your part, I'll take care of the rest.'

'I'll do what I can.' He glanced from her to Juan and she knew what was going on in his mind, drawing a sigh of relief when she realised he wasn't going to press the matter. 'I won't ask who it is you're chasing so determinedly,' he promised. 'If the interview comes off I'll see it in the papers, if not—well, at least I'll have done my bit.'

'And I'll always be grateful to you,' Kristie told him.

Juan brooded silently and after a moment or two Paco swallowed the last of his coffee and prepared to leave them. 'I have to go, but I'll see you both very soon, I expect. When I have any information, Kristie, I'll ring you—O.K.?' She nodded, and he looked down at Juan, then shrugged. 'Don't worry, *amigo*,' he told him cheerfully, 'crazy people have their own protection from harm, eh? *Adios, amigos!*'

After he'd gone Juan still sat with his elbows on the table, gloomy and pessimistic, then he looked across at her, still frowning. 'Is it worth it, Kristie? Taking all this trouble and running such risks?'

'It could be well worth it,' she insisted, anxious to convince him. 'There's a lot riding on this, Juan. My editor expects me to get an interview with Montevio and that's what I'm going to do. He won't care how I go about it, I assure you, as long as he isn't landed with a law-suit!'

He didn't like it at all. Not that she had expected him to, but she was in no mood to change her plan now and with Paco Armandaz's co-operation she could bring it off she felt sure. 'I hadn't realised until now that being a journalist meant going to any lengths and making a cheap exhibition of yourself,' Juan remarked bitterly, and pushing back the hair from her forehead Kristie eyed him reproachfully.

'Is that how you see me?' she asked.

Juan shook his head, his eyes darkly unhappy. 'You know it isn't; but I'm thinking of the impression Montevio will get when he finds you out.'

He was getting to her, but Kristie refused to be deterred. 'With luck he won't find me out,' she told him.

'Not until I'm ready for him, and by then it will be too late for him to do anything. Once I'm inside I shall have to play it by ear, but I'm confident I can handle it; after all, he's only a man like any other man, whatever his reputation.'

Juan sighed, shaking his head at her optimism. 'At least let me come with you, Kristie.'

He was genuinely concerned about her, and she knew it. He was a very good friend as well as her second cousin, and she was fond of him, and it was quite instinctive when she reached over and placed her hand over his, giving him a small rueful smile. 'I'd rather you didn't, Juan, although I appreciate your motives, but I honestly believe I can handle this better on my own. Once Paco has set up the van driver for me I'm half-way there.'

'Once you're inside those grounds you've only just begun,' Juan prophesied gloomily, and she squeezed his hand in an attempt to cheer him up.

'You're being an unnecessary pessimist,' she told him, 'but I'll make allowances, because I know how you feel.'

Juan gazed at her for a moment with sombre dark eyes, and she caught a glimpse of something that she had never seen there before. Turning his hand over, he clasped hers tightly for a moment. 'I don't think you do,' he said softly, and Kristie wondered uneasily if she might not have to take a long hard look at her situation with Juan before too long.

CHAPTER TWO

KRISTIE found obtaining the necessary clothes easy enough, but making herself into a passable boy was a little more difficult than she had anticipated, she had to admit. The final result was tolerable, but not as good as she had hoped, and there seemed nothing she could do about a tight and definitely nauseous feeling in her stomach.

It was mostly excitement, she kept telling herself, but in her innermost heart she had to admit there was apprehension too. Ever since Paco Armandaz had telephoned with the news that their firm did indeed deliver to the Villa de los Naranjos, and that he had arranged with the driver to take her on his next trip, she had been as jumpy as a flea. Only pride and stubbornness kept her from having a change of heart; that and the determination to make the most of a situation she could never hope to have repeated.

It was convenient that Aunt Maria had chosen to go shopping in the city, so that Juan was alone in the *salón* when Kristie presented herself for inspection. To her dismay she was shivering with mingled excitement and apprehension, and her eyes were unnaturally bright below the peak of the cap she wore. Her voice quavered slightly too as she invited his opinion.

A pair of second-hand grey trousers had been chosen deliberately because their ill-fitting bagginess suggested they were hand-me-downs, and in no way could they have been termed flattering, while a fawn coarse cotton shirt hung loosely enough to completely hide any suggestion of femininity. As it was the height of summer she had been obliged to dispense with the added concealment that a jacket would have afforded, but a cap was essential.

Few Spanish males wore hats except on festive occasions, but Kristie had to be an exception. She had chosen a wide-topped leather cap to cover her mass of black hair and wore it pulled well down over her forehead to hide as much of her face as possible. Not even among the handsome Andaluz was one likely to see quite such a pretty boy.

'How do I look?'

She waited for Juan's opinion with a certain air of bravado, and he studied her for a moment in silence. 'Exactly like a very pretty girl dressed in boy's clothes,' he informed her, and Kristie gave an impatient shake of her head.

'Oh, don't be such a pessimist,' she told him. 'Why don't you give me some encouragement instead of trying to make it harder for me?'

'Because I wish you'd give up this crazy idea before it's too late—please, Kristie.'

'I can't.' The quiver in her voice showed how disappointed she was in him, and her eyes were reproachfully brilliant below the deep peak of the leather cap. 'Please don't try to undermine my confidence, Juan, it's hard enough as it is.'

Once more he regarded her steadily for a moment, then he came across and took a firm grip on her arms, looking down into her face with a disturbing intensity. 'I wish you luck, but only because I daren't think what might happen to you if this doesn't work,' he said, and drew her to him, touching her mouth lightly with his for a moment. 'Good luck, my little pigeon,' he murmured softly. 'And in God's name be careful.'

He said little while they walked to where she was to rendezvous with the driver of the van, and she knew just how reluctantly he watched her go. Nor was the driver a very willing accomplice, as she soon discovered, for he lost no time letting her know his opinion. 'I don't know what it is you have in mind, *señorita*,' he informed her, 'but I want you to know that I'm doing this only because young Señor Armandaz asked me to. I can't see why a legitimate visitor can't call in the usual way. Señora de

Mena is a very charming lady as well as a good customer, and if she were to find out——'

'Señora de Mena?'

Kristie interrupted him sharply, and the man frowned. 'Is it not her house you're trying to get into?' he asked. 'The Villa de los Naranjos, Señor Armandaz told me; you want to see the *señora*'s son I was told.'

'Have *you* ever seen him?' Kristie asked anxiously, and the man shrugged.

'He's a writer, I'm told; he's most likely busy when I call. I've never seen him, only the *señora*, his mother; a very kind and polite lady.' It must be that Manuel Montevio's mother had remarried, Kristie decided, for there couldn't be any mistake; she had seen him for herself. 'If my own daughter behaved in such a way,' the man went on, 'pursuing a man into the privacy of his home, I'd see to it that she regretted it!'

Her cheeks flushed, Kristie took the criticism because she had little option in the circumstances, but she felt as if there was no one in sympathy with her as the van made its way through the streets of Seville to the more outlying districts. 'I very likely will regret it if anything goes wrong,' she told him, and glanced at the stolid country face from the corner of her eye. 'I can understand your feelings to some extent, *señor*, and I'm grateful for your co-operation in the circumstances. If there was some other way I could reach Señor—Señora de Mena's son I'd take it, believe me. But there isn't, and this is very important to me.'

The man merely nodded, but somehow Kristie got the impression that he might have been won over just a little. They were driving through the countryside now and she gave her attention to what she had to do when they arrived at the villa. She must remain undetected, at least initially, until she could decide on a course of action, and then it would be in the lap of the gods what happened.

She missed Juan's company more than she had expected to, and she wondered why it only now occurred to her that he could, with a little coaching, have taken the driver's place and at least been there to lend his moral support, if nothing else. But it was too late now to have regrets, for they were following the same narrow country road she had come with Juan. And with the same startling suddenness a sharp bend in the road brought the Villa de los Naranjos into sight just ahead.

Her heart was hammering hard in her breast and she was shaking like a leaf, she realised. Yet she suffered a moment of alarm when the van went straight on past the locked gate; until she realised that tradesmen would not go calling at the main entrance to a property like the Villa de los Naranjos.

In fact the driver followed a narrow track that ran below the high *patio* wall surrounding the property, and pulled up beside a small wooden gate set in the wall at the rear of the house. 'Tradesmen's entrance,' he informed her with a hint of malice. 'Now you go your own way, *señorita*.'

She got out of the van and stood for a moment looking up at the height of the wall. 'How long have I got?' she asked, and the shaky sound of her own voice came as a shock.

The man paused in opening the rear door of the van and eyed her shrewdly. 'You think you'll be coming back with me?'

Grappling with her growing nervousness, Kristie swallowed hard. 'It depends how long I am, naturally,' she said, 'and I can't hold you up. So if I don't show up by the time you're ready to leave, don't wait.'

Broad shoulders humped a box of groceries from the van, and he turned to open the gate. 'I won't,' he promised grimly.

There was no one about when Kristie made her way along the back of the house, taking advantage of every scrap of cover afforded by thick shrubs and shadowy trees, and she thanked heaven for their shade as she headed for the corner of the house, with no definite purpose in mind as yet. It alarmed her to realise just how nervous she was, and her heartbeat almost deafened her as she stood for a moment in the shade of a huge hibiscus considering her next move.

The leather cap was uncomfortably hot, but she kept the peak pulled firmly down over her forehead as she looked around her, and she almost literally jumped out of her skin when a man's voice spoke just behind her. 'Who are you, and what the devil are you doing here?' the voice demanded.

The peak of the cap had slipped down until it covered even her brows and she was too startled to remember her role of errand boy. Her first instinct was to run, but even while she was trying desperately to keep panic in check, a large hand fastened itself about her upper arm and swung her round.

'Answer me, damn you!'

He sounded so angry that escape was the only thing she could think of and, responding to instinct, she abandoned the opportunity of a face-to-face confrontation and yielded to sheer panic. She was free and running, but as she turned the corner of the house she almost collided with someone coming from the opposite direction, vaguely recognising it as female by the cry of surprise.

She felt trapped, with the newcomer blocking her way of escape and Manuel Montevio following close on her heels, looking so fiercely stern that she shivered. She was trembling from head to foot and her heart was thudding wildly, though she condemned herself for a coward, and she started nervously when the woman spoke.

'What is this, Manuel?'

'We have an intruder, Mama!'

'Oh, surely not?' The woman frowned at him worriedly. 'But how, with all the precautions we take?' she asked, and Manuel Montevio made a sharp, impatient sound very like a snarl.

'That's exactly what I mean to find out!' he told her, and shook Kristie so hard that her teeth rattled. 'Now, you miserable little wretch, how did you get in? Answer me!'

He was so angry that even the woman he had addressed

as Mama reproached him. 'There's surely no need to be quite so cruel, Manuel,' she protested, and from her appearance and her softly persuasive voice, Kristie took her to be the van driver's charming and polite Señora de Mena.

She was tall and brown-haired, and Kristie took hope from the glimpse she had of gentle brown eyes. She dared not study her too long for fear of giving herself away, but she noted that the face was gentle too, and softly feminine. In fact she probably represented Kristie's one hope of escaping her son's vengeance, and she thanked heaven for her arrival.

'This child hardly presents much of a threat,' the woman went on, 'and you look fierce enough to terrify anyone, my son.'

'I mean to,' Manuel Montevio told her darkly. 'In fact, Mama, this—this child, as you call her, is a reporter.'

'Oh no, I can't believe it!'

The brown eyes looked unhappy, probably knowing from experience that he would be proved right, and Kristie had the horrible feeling that she had already been recognised as one of the passengers in the car that had blocked his exit a few days earlier. 'I've seen this particular specimen before,' he went on, 'although God knows how she discovered where I was.'

The woman was evidently still taking Kristie at face value, for she looked at him curiously. 'She?'

'This is no boy,' her son declared harshly. 'Take a look!'

Kristie cried out in protest, but there was nothing she could do to avoid the hand that reached round and grabbed a handful of her shirt at the back, taking up the concealing folds and pulling the front taut against her body so that her sex was no longer in doubt. Not content with that, he gave a sharp tug that broke the thread on several of the flimsily attached buttons and allowed the two halves of the front to gape, exposing the unmistakably feminine swell of her breasts.

'Manuel!'

The protest came from the older woman, but it went

unheeded as, still grasping the loose back of her shirt, he jerked Kristie round to face him. She dared not raise her head to glare at him, but she pulled vainly at the two halves of her shirt front while still keeping her head down, and he held her with an ease that was almost contemptuous. His free hand held in such a way that she half expected to feel its weight on her cheek.

She couldn't see his face, only in a fleeting glimpse from below the peak of her cap, but she got an impression of a dark grey suit and a white shirt, with a glimpse of brown throat at the open neck, and her heart beat wildly in alarm. A man like any other, she had told Juan, but Manuel Montevio was proving himself to be a man like no other she had ever met, and he alarmed her as she had never been alarmed before.

'So you came back in spite of my warning!' He shook her again, and again it was hard enough to rattle her teeth and make her breathless. She was horribly aware of how vulnerable her near-nakedness made her, and she was dismayed to realise that she simply didn't know how to cope with the situation. 'What did you hope to achieve with this—masquerade?' he demanded.

'To find a way into this place and see you, and I did!' Even now she could feel some small triumph at having made her point, but she was too conscious of being half undressed to enjoy it for long. 'Please,' she went on breathlessly, 'let me go. You're pulling my shirt, and— please!'

Her obvious discomfort obviously had no effect on him at all, and it wasn't going to do her any good appealing to him. Twisting the soft material tighter in his hand, he let his eyes linger for a moment, very deliberately, on the soft curve of her breast, and the bold, dark fierceness of his gaze touched her like a physical assault.

'You're embarrassed?' he asked in a voice that was suddenly purringly soft. 'You surprise me, *señorita*! I thought your breed were beyond any kind of human decency!'

Above the wild, thudding urgency of her heart, Kristie

heard the older woman murmur some kind of reproach. But anger was beginning to replace fear and embarrassment and she set her mouth into a firm line, though still keeping her head down, keeping her face hidden as far as possible. 'You're a fine one to talk of human decency!' she retorted, and began to try and wriggle free of him until she realised she was simply making the situation worse by drawing attention to what she wanted to conceal. 'You have no right to treat me like this—I simply wanted to have a few words with you——'

'And I made it quite clear that I hadn't the slightest wish to talk to you or any of your kind,' he interrupted relentlessly. 'I don't know how you got in here, but I'm within my rights in sending for the *guardia* and having you arrested for trespass!'

Just as Juan had warned her, Kristie thought, and made one last plea, though without much hope of it being heeded. 'But you can't—I'm not a criminal!'

Her own protest coincided with that of the older woman. 'Manuel,' she said quietly, 'that would be unnecessarily harsh, my son.'

He clearly resented the accusation and shook his head firmly. 'I disagree, Mama. I dislike having my privacy invaded by these vultures! If I deal hardly with this one it may serve as a warning and discourage the rest.'

'But a girl,' his mother objected. 'A young girl!'

The soft voice sought to persuade him and, hopeful of its success, Kristie came quickly to her own defence, desperate to salvage at least something of the mission. 'I'm the only one who knows where you are, Señor Montevio,' she assured him anxiously. 'If you just talked to me and——'

'It would bring the whole wolf-pack howling after me,' he declared, and glared at her with hard, amber eyes. 'You forget I've been through this before, *señorita*!'

'Because you were a celebrity,' Kristie insisted huskily. 'People in your position must expect to be followed by the press—you're news.'

'I do not allow that anyone need be hounded because

they appear in the public eye,' he denied harshly. 'You don't convince me, *señorita*, and I don't intend being subjected to the same thing again. Having you locked up for a few days could warn them off!'

He was implacable, and Kristie had almost given up hope of his relenting. She fastened as many of the buttons as remained on her shirt with trembling fingers, while she told him exactly what she thought of him; why not? she had nothing to lose. 'You're cruel, bigoted and unreasonable,' she told him, and got a dizzying moment of satisfaction from turning the tables. Yanking the peak of the cap down far enough to defeat his angry, questing gaze, she went on, 'All I'm asking is a few minutes of your time; no one else knows where you are, I'd swear to it, and this means an awful lot to me, but you won't even listen.'

Swiftly and with unmistakable meaning, his gaze swept over her from head to foot, and again his mouth showed that suggestion of cruelty. 'My time is too valuable to waste on someone like you, *señorita*. You obviously have a poor opinion of my intelligence if you hoped to fool me with that childish disguise, and I don't appreciate being taken for a fool! If you go now, at once, I won't call the *guardia*, but if you don't——'

Señora de Mena's voice broke softly into the unspoken threat. 'Manuel, be reasonable.'

'Reasonable?' He turned to his mother with hot, glittering eyes, as if he resented her criticism as deeply as he did Kristie's presence. 'You know my feelings about reporters, Mama. I won't be harassed again after all this time, and I certainly won't allow myself to be harried by a brassy-haired blonde who's scarcely out of the schoolroom!'

So he remembered her wearing the blonde wig and obviously had no idea of her real colouring, and Kristie was in no mood to enlighten him, she was too intent on following her own wild inclinations. 'I've been long enough out of the schoolroom to have heard of you and your reputation, Señor Montevio,' she said, rashly uncaring. 'I know you've always disliked the press, but I'm wondering why!'

'*Señorita*——'

The whispered caution came from Señora de Mena, but Kristie paid it no heed. 'What do you have to hide?' she insisted, her eyes bright below the peak of the cap that overshadowed them. 'Is there something you were afraid the press would find out about you? Is that why you slipped so suddenly out of sight—because you were afraid they might find out your secret? You can have me thrown off your property, *señor*, but sooner or later I'll find out what made you abandon your career when it was at its peak, and why you choose to hide yourself away behind high walls and locked gates!'

'In God's name, that's enough!'

Something in his voice touched an unexpected chord in her, and Kristie found herself not only breathlessly emotional but with tears in her eyes; nor was she enjoying her moment of retaliation nearly as much as she thought she would. He was a Titan, and she had tried to bring him down but failed miserably, for he still stood there as tall and unyielding as ever, while she was trembling and close to tears.

'Just because you're so young and, I suspect, new to the job,' he said in a voice that was firmly under control once more, 'I'm giving you another chance to leave here before I call the *guardia*; but only one, *señorita*—do I make myself clear?' The tall, sinewy body was drawn up as taut as a bowstring, and once again a brief flick of fear skimmed along her spine. 'Leave now or I'll have you removed!'

Shaking like a leaf, Kristie slid her gaze from his implacable harshness to the woman's gentle and rather anxious face, then she slid the tip of her tongue over her lips. She found it hard to believe that she meant to express regret. 'Señor Montevio——'

She gave an involuntary cry of alarm when she found herself seized firmly by one arm and propelled quickly along the path by which she had come in, panting and

stumbling in the unfamiliar clumsiness of boy's shoes.
Manuel Montevio paid no heed to anything but his own
unyielding purpose, and as she was dragged along towards
the gate Kristie could only hope and pray that she would
not have to walk home after all she had been through.

He pulled open the low wooden gate with his free hand,
and his fingers dug hard into her flesh for a moment. 'I
shan't tell you again,' he declared. 'You and your kind
aren't welcome here—now go!'

She was pushed through the gateway roughly, so off
balance that she only just managed to save herself from
falling, and she grabbed hastily at the few remaining buttons on her shirt when they once more parted company.
Her cap skewed perilously awry so that she grabbed that
with her other hand, and she had not even time to recover
her balance before she heard the vicious slam of the gate
closing.

'Brute!' she yelled at its inhospitable blankness.

Catching sight of the grocery van just disappearing
around the end of the wall was the last straw. Kristie
dropped down on to the ground in the shade of the over-
hanging orange trees and wept in sheer frustration.

The worst thing about having failed so miserably was
having to tell Juan about it, and Kristie put it off as long
as she possibly could. Having avoided the subject most of
the day, however, she had little choice, as they sat together
that evening in their favourite bar, but to be honest about
it.

Only one thing about the whole venture gave her any
satisfaction at all, and that was the knowledge that
Manuel Montevio's defences could be breached by anyone
determined enough to take chances. Facing up to the man
himself, however, was a different matter entirely, and she
had to admit to utter disaster in that direction.

The woman she assumed to be Señora de Mena was
interesting too, for since he claimed her as his mother yet
had a different surname, either the woman had remarried
or there was another, less simple explanation. Manuel

Montevio's dislike of the press's attention could mean that he had something to hide, as Kristie had suggested, though not with that specific meaning in mind.

To be born outside marriage no longer carried the stigma it once had, but Manuel Montevio was a proud man, and she could well imagine how sensitive he would be in such a situation. Not that she had any intention of suggesting it to anyone else, not even Juan, but it did offer a possible reason for his hatred of her profession.

He would more than likely expect her to be warned off after their last encounter, but if that was so then he had a good deal to learn about her. She was a journalist, and a good journalist never gave up on a story; although in her innermost heart Kristie was beginning to wonder if she hadn't taken on more than she could cope with after all. Normally her items were tucked away and lost in the inside pages, and if this story was handled right it could make secondary headlines if not the front page.

'So what happens now?' Juan asked as he refilled her wine glass, and Kristie knew without doubt that he too expected her to have had enough and be ready to give up.

She shrugged, picking a plump and succulent prawn from the dish of *tapas* in front of her and disposing of it with quite unladylike relish before she answered him. 'I shall try again, naturally,' she told him, as if it would be no trouble at all to do just that.

Juan seemed to have momentarily lost his appetite, and he stared at her. 'Are you mad?' he demanded. 'Do you actually enjoy being manhandled and thrown out into the road to make your own way home?'

'No, of course I don't, but I'm not going to give up, and there are more ways of killing a cat, you know.'

'Of killing—a *cat*?' Juan looked at her blankly for a moment, then lifted his hands in appeal. 'Where on earth does a cat come into this? What cat, for the love of heaven?'

Often when she translated English idioms into Spanish she managed to confuse him, although quite frequently he later adopted them for his own use, and Kristie smiled as she popped in another prawn and licked her lips in uninhibited appreciation. 'There are more ways of killing a cat than choking it to death with cream,' she quoted. 'In other words, there's always more than one way of achieving the same end. I didn't get what I wanted this time, but I hope I'll do better next time.'

'Holy Mother!' Juan appealed piously, and looked across at her with a hint of desperation in his eyes. 'Please, Kristie, no more disguises! Why don't you just be a sensible girl and get on with enjoying your holiday, eh? After all, it's why you're here, not to go chasing after a man who obviously doesn't want anything to do with you, and isn't too particular how he lets you know it. Just let it go, Kristie, eh?'

'Behave like a lady, you mean?' Her eyes had the same bright gleam of determination as she selected an olive from the dish and popped it into her mouth. 'Haven't you learned yet, Juan, that I mean to put Montevio back into the news again, whether he likes it or not?'

Juan eyed her broodingly, his brows drawn. 'I'm beginning to sympathise with him,' he declared. 'And trying to keep an eye on you is making me old before my time.'

'Then give it up,' Kristie told him, although secretly she hoped he wouldn't take her advice, for knowing he was always there in the background was a comfort, and she'd really hate it if he did leave her to her own devices.

'You know I can't do that.' He was looking at her with the half appealing, half bold look that she always found so hard to resist. 'But please, Kristie, for my sake will you take more care? While you're staying with me and Madre I feel I'm responsible for you.'

'But you're not! I'm a free agent and nobody need be responsible for me; I'm perfectly capable of looking after myself.'

'Like you did this morning?'

He was worried about her and she could not be other than affected by it, so that she reached over and placed a hand lightly over his. 'Dear Juan,' she said softly, 'I know you mean well, but I don't really need protecting, although I appreciate having you there if I do need a hand. I'm an experienced journalist and used to meeting all sorts of people.'

Nothing would convince Juan, however, and one dark brow questioned her last statement. 'Not men like Montevio,' he insisted. 'I honestly believe he could prove dangerous if you push too hard, Kristie. When I think of the way you looked when you came home today—your shirt torn and your eyes swollen from crying. And to push you out into the road without bothering to ask how you were going to get home—He's out of your league, *chica*, and I wish you'd recognise it.' He regarded her for a moment with his head to one side. 'Or perhaps you do, but you just won't admit it.'

'I won't admit it because it just isn't true,' Kristie declared firmly, and wished she could feel as confident as she sounded. 'Don't worry, Juan, I'll find a way, you'll see.'

Juan pulled a rueful face. 'That's what I'm afraid of,' he said.

Kristie was enjoying a cup of coffee on the *patio* the following morning when her aunt came to find her, and she noticed that the older woman looked both puzzled and a little uneasy. 'There's someone to see you, Kristie,' she told her, and Kristie frowned curiously as she got up.

'Who is it, Aunt Maria?' she asked as she followed her back to the house. 'One of our crowd?'

She and Juan had a lot of friends of both sexes, but they seldom called at one another's homes, preferring to meet in various bars and cafés in the city. 'Someone older,' her aunt assured her. 'And she's a—a lady, Kristie. Do you know what I mean?'

'I think so.' Kristie also had an idea who the caller might be, although it was no more than an inspired guess. 'Is it Señora de Mena?' she asked, but couldn't imagine how the *señora* had tracked her down, or even why she had bothered to try.

'It sounded something like that, but you know I'm getting a little hard of hearing lately, child.'

'But what can she possibly want with me?' Kristie asked, as much of herself as her aunt.

'The easiest way to find that out is to ask her,' Aunt Maria suggested practically. 'She's in the *salón.*'

Kristie came to a halt part way across the hall and she clutched her aunt's arm for a moment while she glanced across in the direction of the *salón.* 'I don't really want to see her, Aunt Maria,' she whispered. 'Could you—would you tell her that I'm not well or something—please?'

Maria Murillo was a placid and practical woman who could cope with virtually any domestic crisis, but she had certain principles that she stuck to firmly, and she fixed her heavy-lidded eyes on Kristie suspiciously. 'I don't know what you and Juan have been up to lately, Kristie,' she said in her firm deep voice, 'but I know there's something. I may be a little hard of hearing, but I'm not stupid, and I've noticed all the whispering and secretiveness between you lately. And now you ask me to lie to a perfect stranger for no good reason that I can see—well, I decline to lie for you!'

'Then just give me a few minutes to fetch a wig I have upstairs,' Kristie pleaded desperately, and her aunt's frown deepened.

'A wig? What have you done that you need to disguise yourself?'

'I've been doing my job!' If she sounded defiant it was because she was on the defensive and concerned about Señora de Mena's reason for seeking her out. 'Please, Aunt, I promise that's all it is, and it's a very important story, only——' Something occurred to her then and she frowned curiously. 'Did she ask for me by name, Aunt Maria?'

Her aunt shook her head. 'She asked if I knew someone called Juan Murillo and of course I said he was my son; then she asked if my niece was also in the house and if you were could she speak with you.'

Kristie wasn't sure why she was relieved to know that

she was still unknown by name, but she turned hurriedly and went dashing upstairs to fetch the blonde wig. Only minutes later she gave it a nervous tug and opened the *salón* door. 'Señora de Mena?' she asked.

The visitor looked exactly as Aunt Maria had described her—a lady in the old-fashioned sense of the word, and she looked so perfectly composed that she made Kristie feel even less sure of herself. She remained on her chair while the gentle dark eyes took in a very different picture of the previous day's intruder, and she frowned slightly.

Kristie was still wearing trousers, but they were well-tailored blue slacks worn with a cream silk blouse, and the blonde wig emphasised the fairness of her skin while at the same time giving a false impression of the shape of her face. It fluffed out at the sides and made her face look much thinner, and completely hid her forehead under a heavy fringe, and the fact that she looked so unlike her natural self gave her a little more confidence.

She still didn't give her own name, and the caller didn't ask for it, but smiled at her a little uncertainly now. 'You *are* the same young lady who called on my son yesterday, *señorita*?' she asked, and Kristie saw no sense in denying it.

Instead of sitting down, she stood by the window with the sun behind her giving the blonde wig a garishly brassy look. 'I tried to get an interview with Señor Montevio,' she agreed. 'As you know, I was unsuccessful. *señora*.'

'May I ask how you knew where he was to be found?'

The question was gentle but probing, and Kristie felt a moment's unease. 'I—I heard,' was as far as she committed herself. 'Someone saw him and recognised him.'

'And told you?'

'Not actually,' Kristie confessed. 'I just heard it and decided to do something about it—it's what I'm paid for, after all.'

'Of course. You were roughly handled and I'm sorry about that, but your methods were rather unorthodox, *señorita*, you must agree.'

'I'd already tried a more orthodox approach,' Kristie told her, 'but it didn't work, so I was forced to try something a bit more—devious.'

'Because it's important for you to interview my son?'

'I'm the only one so far who knows where he is,' Kristie told her, 'and he's news whether he likes it or not, *señora*.'

'And you are determined to have an exclusive, so you won't let up.'

'I don't want to—to hound him,' Kristie insisted, 'but I need this break, *señora*, it's important to me. Do you understand?'

This kindly woman was the antithesis of her forceful son and she invited confidence. 'I understand, *señorita*, but I'm afraid my son never will. I came to see you for a reason you will possibly find hard to understand.' She hesitated, her elegant hands clasped tightly together in her anxiety. 'I came to make a personal plea; to try and persuade you to give up the idea of interviewing Manuel and let him remain in obscurity as he wishes.'

It was an appeal that was hard to resist, but Kristie hung on grimly to her advantage. She hated to refuse this charming and gentle woman, but she determinedly hardened her heart against yielding. 'I'm sorry, *señora*,' she said in a voice that was not quite steady, 'but I can't do it.'

'You thought him unforgivably harsh?' Señora de Mena suggested, and Kristie wondered how she could be expected to think him otherwise.

'Surely you have to agree he was,' she challenged. 'Maybe Señor Montevio has his own reasons for behaving as he did, but you must see that it didn't exactly invite my sympathy. And it certainly didn't make me any less determined to get an interview one way or another; I can't give up, *señora*, I'm sorry.'

For a moment the dark eyes added their appeal, then she sighed and got slowly to her feet, while Kristie carefully avoided her eyes. 'I suppose not,' she allowed, though with obvious regret. 'But I would ask you, *señorita*, to deal more kindly with my son than he has with you. It must be hard for you to understand, but Manuel is an intensely private person, and his dislike of the press stems from that, it is a—a kind of shyness, although you no doubt find that hard to believe. He'll never give you an interview, but it occurs to me that you might write a feature on him without the personal contact, and in that case I implore you to be fair in your assessment. Will you do that, *señorita?*'

It was an appeal that was too hard to resist, and Kristie was still a little dazed at the thought of Manuel Montevio being shy; it was too much to believe and surely the imaginings of a doting mother. Nevertheless she could see no harm in putting her mind at rest on one point at least. 'You have my word that I won't write anything that isn't the truth, *señora*, I promise you that. It wouldn't be—ethical.'

It wasn't quite the answer she sought, and briefly the soft dark eyes regarded her anxiously. 'I must trust you to be both fair and truthful, *señorita*,' she said, and offered her hand with a faint smile. 'It's a pity we couldn't have met in happier circumstances.'

It made Kristie uneasy to realise that she had a genuine liking for her, and she could not imagine how someone like Señora de Mena had borne such a harsh and autocratic son. He must surely be like his father, whoever he might be. It was only as she opened the outer gate for her caller that Kristie thought to enquire how she had found her.

As she stood in the gateway the shadows of the trees fell across her face and added lines and angles to the gentle features, making it difficult to judge her reaction. But her eyes looked more shrewd than Kristie had seen them so far, as she explained.

'Unlike my son I had little difficulty in guessing that your mysterious arrival had coincided with the delivery of the groceries from Armandaz, and I've known old Jorge long enough for him to trust me. He wasn't happy about his part in it, but I promised not to give him away, and he in turn told me that you were the cousin of a friend of young Señor Armandaz. He told me which district he had picked you up in and from Armandaz senior I learned that his son had only two friends in that area—a young man named Juan Murillo and his cousin, whose name he didn't know. It was a gamble, *señorita*, but as you see I'm as adept as you are at tracking down my quarry.'

'And will you tell him—your son?'

The older woman shook her head. 'I've no more wish for him to come here bent on vengeance than you are, my dear *señorita*; I shan't tell him.'

'Thank you, *señora*.'

She seemed in less hurry to leave suddenly, and she studied Kristie for a moment before she spoke. 'I think you might be a very nice girl behind that façade of hard-headed reporter,' she observed, and smiled faintly as she turned to go. A liveried chauffeur held open the door of a huge black limousine for her and she turned back briefly as she got in, her dark eyes gently mocking for a moment. 'And I'm sure you're much prettier without that awful wig—*Adios, señorita!*'

Kristie was left staring after her departing car and feeling rather foolish, then with a shrug she turned back into the gardens, pulling off the offending wig and glaring at it in disgust. It had been a stupid idea and Señora de Mena had evidently seen through the attempt at disguise more easily than her son had done, for he had referred to her as a brassy-haired blonde.

She hadn't gone far when Juan came hurrying to meet her, his eyes avid with curiosity. 'You've had a visitor,' he said, obviously having got the information from his mother. 'How on earth did she know where to find you, Kristie?'

'Oh, she has her sources of information just as I have.' She shrugged, declining to enlighten him further. 'She's very nice, Juan, I liked her.'

'What did she want?'

Kristie turned across the *patio*, for she had no desire to face Aunt Maria's questions as well. In as few words as possible she explained Señora de Mena's motive for coming, and also assured him that the *señora* had given her word not to let her son know where they lived, though Juan looked unconvinced.

'You might be less ready to trust her when you hear what I have to say,' he told her, and sat down facing her across the table. 'Kristie, I've discovered that they're descended from the Borgias.'

It was so unexpected and so bizarre an announcement that she simply stared at him. 'What on earth are you talking about?'

'Paco got interested in them after your little escapade, and he discovered, though don't ask me how, that Señora de Mena came here from Játiva, up near Valencia. Apparently he'd talked to someone who knew her family, although nothing much about her personally, and they're descended from a branch of the Borgia family. They were big in that part of the world a few hundred years ago, you know—the Borgia Pope and his evil brood started there.'

'I don't see how it has any bearing on my problem,' Kristie told him, 'but I can't say I'm surprised.' Then it occurred to her that the information would at least fill in a useful gap in the so far blank background of Manuel Montevio. 'I can't see Señora de Mena as one of them, but her son, yes. Cesare Borgia was the nastiest of them all, and he had red hair too! Well,' she amended after a second's consideration, 'red-gold really; it's an interesting combination with amber-coloured eyes.'

'Has he got amber eyes?' Juan asked, and she answered without hesitation.

'Red-gold hair, gold eyelashes, a golden skin, golden eyes; no wonder they called him the Golden Spaniard! He's very eye-catching.'

'And attractive?' Juan suggested quietly.

'Very!' She glanced at him from the corner of her eyes and sought hastily to banish any idea that she was softening towards her quarry. 'He's also a bully and an arrogant, overbearing tyrant!'

'And a Borgia,' Juan reminded her. 'They were a dangerous lot, Kristie, have you forgotten?'

Kristie shrugged. 'There's not much scope for wholesale poisonings and garrottings these days,' she told him, and looked across at him with a faint smile. 'I shan't give up, Juan, so it's no use trying to frighten me off.'

'I realise that,' Juan said glommily. 'I only wish I could.'

CHAPTER THREE

It wasn't very often that Kristie had the opportunity to take out Juan's car on her own, but as he had gone out with friends and didn't need it she had decided to take advantage of it and go for a drive. Her pursuit of Manuel Montevio had reached stalemate, for she simply couldn't think of any way to get to him, and consequently she was feeling rather restless.

The heat was intense and she had it in mind to drive north towards the cool of the Sierra Morena, for the quiet mountain roads appealed to her. She always felt that the grandeur of the scenery helped to put everything into perspective, and she needed something like that at the moment. The gleam of the river winked and beckoned to her as she approached a tiny village in the foothills, and she was completely relaxed as she drove along the narrow dusty road.

A handful of men working the inhospitable soil spared her an appreciative look and a wave as she drove past them, and she began to feel as if she hadn't a care in the world. The green cotton dress she wore was sleeveless but fairly high-necked, and the skirt was pushed thigh-high for coolness, her feet small and neat in comfortable light sandals. She wore her long black hair loose but held back from her face by a green silk scarf, and her eyes were concealed behind dark glasses, for the sun was fierce when it was reflected off the bonnet of the car.

The village was no more than half a dozen little white *barracas* each within its minuscule *patio*, and she had driven through it in a matter of seconds. It was as she was taking the last sharp bend that she realised she was on a collision course with another car and she hastily swerved to one side at the same time as she slapped her foot on the brake.

How exactly it happened, she couldn't be sure, but she must have been closer to the *patio* wall surrounding the last little cottage than she realised. There was a hideous scraping noise, then the little car juddered alarmingly before coming to an abrupt halt that jerked her forward in her seat and brought her head into contact with the windscreen.

Dazedly she registered the sound of a car door slamming, followed by the rapid approach of heavy footsteps, then she quite suddenly lost interest. Her moment of unconsciousness must have been very brief, however, for she came to to find herself being lifted from behind the wheel by a pair of strong arms, and a brief, light brush of fingers on her thigh suggested that her skirt was being lowered, but the sensation was so comforting that she immediately closed her eyes again.

Whoever he was, he was taking her into the *barraca* whose wall she had hit, she guessed, for the coolness of its interior was a blessed relief after the heat of the sun. 'On here, *señor*,' a woman's voice murmured, and Kristie was gently laid on to some kind of bed or settee. She almost stopped breathing altogether when she heard the man's voice, for it was unmistakable and the last one she had expected to hear on this quiet mountain road.

'Have you some fresh cold water, *señora*, please?' he asked, and even the soft-voiced request held a certain command, Kristie noted dizzily.

Her heart was thudding and added to an overall feeling of weakness, so that when she opened her eyes it was no more than a fraction. She was still wearing her dark glasses and they might have prevented him from realising she was conscious. The woman was absent for the moment, presumably fetching the water he had asked for, and it was possible through the narrow slits between her lashes to see something of his expression.

It was the first time Kristie had seen him other than in a fury of temper, and his face looked more youthful because of it, although he must have been in his middle thirties. Heavy-lidded eyes seemed to be studying her intently, causing a wary, fluttering beat in her heart in case he recognised her; and she almost gave herself away by flinching when he reached and gently removed the dark glasses, instinctively closing her eyes again.

He continued his study of her for several moments and, although she couldn't see him, the intensity of his gaze was as affecting as a physical touch. Then he put out a hand and lightly touched her forehead, so lightly that she found it hard to believe the same hand had so forcibly propelled her along his garden path and hurled her out on to the road.

There must have been a bruise there, for she gave an involuntary wince when he touched it and at the same time opened her eyes wide and looked up at him. He actually smiled, something she would have said he was incapable of until now, and the effect of it was so stunning that she hastily turned her eyes away and looked around the dim little room instead.

'Ah, good, you've come round,' he said, and it was obvious he was relieved. 'I was beginning to think you were more seriously hurt than I thought. How do you feel, *señorita*? Is your head very painful? Should we send for a doctor for you?'

'Oh no, really, I don't need a doctor.'

Her voice was husky and not quite steady, and Kristie caught her breath when he slid a hand behind her and raised her slightly, at the same time taking the glass of water he had asked for from an elderly woman dressed in the traditional country black. While he supported her with one hand the other pressed the cool glass to her lips, persuading her to drink.

'Please drink some of it, eh?'

There was a purr of softness in his voice that she had noticed in Señora de Mena's but not in his before, and she obediently parted her lips and took a sip of the water. It was cool and she drank deeply, ignoring any possibility of it being impure, for her brain was spinning in confusion as she tried to tell herself that he really hadn't recognised her.

It was feasible when she considered it, for the first time he had had very little opportunity to know what she really looked like with a blonde wig covering her hair and only half her face visible around the windscreen. On the second occasion she had been dressed in boy's clothes with a cap concealing what he presumably still thought of as blonde hair. It was perfectly logical that neither connected in his mind with a long-haired and very feminine brunette.

Briefly she put her hand over his and pushed the glass away. 'Thank you, I feel much better now, *señor*.'

But her head ached and it was instinctive when she put a tentative hand to her forehead, closing her eyes for a second as she did. 'You must have hit your head on the windscreen when you hit the wall, I think,' he told her, and once more that large and gentle hand was laid on her throbbing brow. 'Are you certain I shouldn't fetch a doctor for you, *señorita*? Do you feel dizzy, or sick?'

Kristie gave him a faint smile. 'I've just got a bit of a headache, that's all,' she insisted. 'I wouldn't dream of bothering a doctor, I'm perfectly all right, *señor*, thank you.'

The woman stood at the foot of the cot-bed and seemed very impressed with both her visitors, although obviously Manuel Montevio impressed her most, confirming Kristie's opinion that he was a natural-born autocrat, whatever his behaviour in this instance. Until he straightened up suddenly she hadn't realised that he had been crouched almost double beside her, and was probably very uncomfortable, and that she felt was quite unlike the man she thought she knew.

Now that he stood so toweringly tall in the low-ceilinged room the shadows made it seem as if his features had been etched in strong lines below that distinctive red-gold hair, and Kristie found her senses responding quite alarmingly to him. He wore no jacket and a white shirt showed up a lean sinewy frame as well as the intriguing shadow of golden skin through its texture. He had lean hips and long, powerful-looking legs that were shown off with as much effect as good tailoring could achieve, as he stood with his feet slightly apart in a commanding stance that Kristie felt was typical of the side of his character she was more familiar with. No one could deny that he was a very virile and attractive man—least of all Kristie in her present situation.

'If you feel a little stronger would you like to try standing?'

Kristie came swiftly back to earth and gave a slight nod, something she regretted immediately as she clasped a hand to her aching head. In a moment he was crouched beside her again, and a big gentle hand laid lightly on her brow. 'That was very unwise,' he scolded softly, and put a hand either side of her face for a moment while he looked into her eyes. 'Is it very bad? *Should* you see a doctor, *señorita*?'

Kristie did her best to smile, but there was something so incredibly disturbing about the touch of his hands that made her feel even more dizzy than the effects of the accident. 'No, I'm fine, honestly; I just have to remember not to nod my head!'

'Take it very slowly, eh?'

She almost nodded again, then remembered and half-smiled instead as she lay back, prepared to let him take the lead, whatever he decided. Her dark blue eyes looked up at him from the shadow of black lashes, and just for a moment she caught a glimpse of something in the gaze that met hers, that she found hard to believe. It was so startling and unexpected that the throbbing pulse at her temple began to beat with new urgency.

'I think it might be better if you stayed here and rested for a few more minutes while I go and check on your car, O.K.?'

Kristie hastily checked another nod and half smiled instead. 'I'm hindering you, *señor*,' she murmured. 'Please don't let me delay you any longer.'

'You expect me to drive off and leave you like this?' For a moment the frown and the imperious question reminded her of how different he could be, and she caught her lip between her teeth anxiously. 'I wouldn't dream of it,' he insisted. 'If your car has been damaged badly it will have to be towed away, but if it isn't too bad I'm sure the *señora* will agree to let it remain where it is until you can collect it.' An enthusiastic nod confirmed his belief, and he went on as if he had never had any doubt, 'If you'll tell me where you were going, *señorita*, I'll drive you there.'

Suddenly faced with a new possibility, Kristie hesitated. 'It—it's very kind of you, *señor*, but really——'

'I insist!'

That was so much more like the Manuel Montevio she was used to that for a moment Kristie's heart missed a beat. She couldn't cope with his more aggressive side at the moment, so she hastily sought to appease him, though she blamed herself for a coward. 'You're very kind,' she murmured meekly, and having got his way, he nodded and once more straightened himself up, standing for a moment and looking down at her.

'I'll only be a few minutes checking on your car,' he told her. 'You stay where you are meanwhile, and when I come back you can tell me where I can drive you to.'

What choice had she? Kristie thought, watching that broad back disappear through the low doorway, and gave herself up to relaxing for a few minutes more. In fact it wasn't too uncomfortable lying there on the small hard cot in the cool and she did relax for a time until she began to realise just what could happen during the drive back to Seville.

She supposed it could be looked upon as an unexpected opportunity to have his exclusive and undivided attention, but as far as she could see that presented more drawbacks than advantages. If he discovered who she really was she could almost believe he would stop the car and order her out leaving her to walk home as she had been obliged to do from the Villa de los Naranjos, and she wasn't feeling up to that at the moment. Yet she didn't see how she could avoid going with him now.

'It isn't too bad at all!' He was back and standing over her once more, looking down with those deep and disturbingly expressive eyes. 'Just a few dents and scratches, that's all, that won't take much to put right.'

Kristie's smile was a little forced, like her sigh of relief. 'Thank goodness for that! It isn't my car, I borrowed it from my cousin, and he'd have been very upset if I'd knocked his car about too badly.'

His gaze was steady between thick golden lashes, and a certain purring softness in his voice shivered over every nerve in her body. 'I'm sure he'd have been much more upset if you'd been badly knocked about, Señorita——?'

'Roderigo.' She answered quickly and a little breathlessly, giving herself no time to even consider telling him a false name, and he inclined his head as he reached down to take her hand.

'I'm called Hernandez, Señorita Roderigo,' he said, and passed of his own falsehood as blandly as if long practice had accustomed him to it, as she supposed it had. 'Manuel Hernandez; how do you do?'

His hard fingers closed tightly over hers for a moment, and Kristie wondered why she should feel such a sense of disappointment because he had given her a false name. Common sense should have told her that it was what he would do if he wanted to go on keeping his real identity a secret, yet she couldn't help wishing he had been frank with her.

The owner of the cottage stood at the foot of the cot still and seemed to be regarding them with a certain air of benevolent approval, as if she suspected this chance meeting would prove to be the forerunner of something more interesting. The wonder was to Kristie that she didn't recognise her renowned countryman, but then she probably had little or no access to the media and knew nothing about sporting personalities, however famous.

'You'll try to stand now, eh?'

Again Manuel's voice broke into her thoughts, and Kristie realised he was holding out both his hands for hers. In her eagerness to prove how fit she was, she moved too quickly and swayed with a sudden slight dizziness as she came upright. 'I'm all right,' she hastened to assure him, but even so she found her legs alarmingly shaky when she put her feet to the floor, and she clung to his supporting hands tightly.

He drew her up slowly, but her unsteadiness as she came upright made her sway again for a moment and she was brought into sudden and unexpected contact with the lean hardness of his body. At once an arm slid across her back and pressed her close, while long hard fingers curved intimately into the warmth of her breast.

'I'm sorry!'

She whispered the apology, her cheek brushed by the startling familiarity of a vee of bronzed flesh in the opening of his shirt, and just briefly she felt the pressure of his fingers in a disturbingly intimate touch. It seemed like an incredibly long time before he eased her away from him very slightly and looked down into her face with eyes that burned as fiercely as she had ever seen them, though not with anger in this instance.

'You seem very unsteady,' he said quietly. 'It's as well you had the good sense to let me drive you, my dear Señorita Roderigo.' Kristie didn't remark on the wisdom of a decision that had to all intents been made for her, but she used her own hands to gently ease farther away from him while noting how reluctantly he relaxed his hold on her. 'Do you feel like going yet?' he asked. 'I'm sure if you don't the *señora*——'

'Oh no, I'm perfectly all right, really.'

He still kept a light hold on her, as if he was reluctant to let her go altogether, and when Kristie recalled how roughly he had treated her on that last occasion at the Villa de los Naranjos, she found it hard to believe this was the same man. Then he had dragged her forcibly through the gardens before evicting her into the road, now his hands rested lightly on the curve of her waist, while he gazed down at her bowed head with a curious gentleness in his eyes.

'And where exactly do I take you, Señorita Roderigo?' he asked softly.

Only now did it occur to Kristie that she didn't want

him to deliver her to her aunt's door, and after a hasty and rather confused review of the situation, she took what she saw as the easiest way out. 'If you're going to Seville, *señor*, you can drop me by the Hotel Seville if you will.'

'An hotel?' He looked puzzled and not very pleased for a moment, then apparently saw reason in her request. 'Ah, you don't want to be compromised by my driving you to your home; yes, I think I understand. Very well, Señorita Roderigo, I'll do as you say.'

Kristie made no attempt to correct his impression, partly because she supposed it was a correct one to some extent. She didn't want to be compromised by having him drive her to her home, because she would rather he didn't know where she lived. 'Thank you, *señor*,' she said meekly, and distinctly heard their almost forgotten hostess give a deep sigh of regret.

'I'll go and fetch the car round while you stay here out of the sun, I'm quite sure the *señora* won't mind your company for a few more minutes, will you, *señora*?' He gave her a faint but frankly disarming smile and clasped her hand firmly. 'Thank you, *señora*, you've been very kind.'

The *señora*, Kristie thought, barely refrained from dropping him a curtsey, and she added her own thanks as Manuel went striding once more through the low doorway. Catching the woman's eye it was irresistible to pass some remark. 'A very forceful man,' she observed, and the woman nodded enthusiastic agreement, baring two rows of big yellow teeth in a beaming smile.

'A real man, eh?' she said with evident relish. '*And* good-looking!'

Kristie couldn't deny it, but she found the distinct lurch that her heart gave when she heard Manuel's car come around the end of the cottage quite alarming. It wasn't at all the kind of reaction she expected where he was concerned. 'Not bad,' she conceded, and coloured furiously when the woman nudged her and chuckled.

His tall figure blocked the doorway for a second, then he slid a hand under her arm and curved his fingers into her flesh so that she caught her breath. 'Shall we go?' he asked, and turned to give the woman watching them a formal salute. '*Adios, señora!*'

Kristie was treated to another huge, yellow-toothed smile and the dark eyes below their sparse brows twinkled with mischief. 'Good luck, *señorita*,' she whispered hoarsely and with such obvious meaning that Kristie turned away hastily.

Sinking back into her seat, she sighed inwardly at her own cowardice, but decided there was nothing to do but say as little as possible and hope not to give herself away. What Juan would have to say about it she didn't even bother to guess at that point.

Obviously Juan was puzzled, and Kristie herself wished her explanation made more sense. Whether or not he was in agreement with her pursuit of Manuel Montevio, Juan wouldn't understand why she had driven all the way back to Seville without taking advantage of the situation, and he would expect something more than the simple tale she had told his mother.

That was why she had decided against cancelling their evening date, and given Juan the real story while they ate a late evening meal in a café. 'He knows my name,' she told him, and once more regretted her slow thinking on that occasion. 'There was no time to think of giving him a false one, it happened too quickly and I hadn't time to think, so I told him the truth. Which is more than he did; he introduced himself as Hernandez—Manuel Hernandez.'

'Which is the name Marcos was given when he went for the interview for the secretarial job,' Juan reminded her. 'At least now we know for sure that it's the same man.'

'He lied without actually telling a lie,' Kristie recalled, and could still wax indignant at the idea of Manuel Montevio being quicker thinking than she had been herself. 'What he said was—I'm called Hernandez, which is true according to Marcos Francisco, although it isn't his name.'

'And he also knows where you live,' said Juan, and looked at her curiously when she shook her head.

'I got him to drop me in town, then took a taxi the rest of the way home.'

'Mother of God!' Juan breathed exasperatedly. 'You're both as devious as the devil! Don't either of you ever think of being straightforward?'

'It pays to be careful with a man like that,' Kristie insisted. She was annoyed with Juan for being so critical. 'That was why I didn't say a word coming home in case I gave myself away. If he'd got even an inkling of who I really was I wouldn't have put it past him to have stopped the car and dumped me at the side of the road, however awful I was feeling!'

Juan's dark eyes studied her for a moment thoughtfully, and his lip was pursed. 'Is he really as much a monster as you make him sound?' he asked, and Kristie's shrug was vaguely defensive.

'When I was trying to do my job he was a perfect horror,' she told him 'but to the girl he almost collided with on the mountain road he was very different. Quiet, kind, gentle even—I could hardly believe it was the same man. Although,' she went on hastily in case he suspected a change of heart, 'even in that situation he had to show his authority. He asked the woman to bring him some water for me as if he had every right to order her around in her own house, and he insisted he was going to drive me home whatever I thought about it. He's just a natural born autocrat.'

For a moment, while she remembered the very different aspect of Manuel Montevio, she sat contemplating the half-consumed omelette on her plate while Juan got on with his meal. 'Does this mean that you're finally admitting he's too much for you?' he asked hopefully, but Kristie shook her head.

'Definitely not! I'm simply waiting for the right opportunity.'

'You had that already,' Juan reminded her quietly, and she again shook her head.

'That was different. Next time will be when I feel more like tackling him and I'll think of something.' She sat with her chin in her hand, her meal completely forgotten, and stared into space. 'If only there was some way I could get into the house! Maybe I could get a job there, in the kitchens or something, then I'd be on the spot.'

'You get worse!' Juan retorted. 'And risk being handed over to the *guardia*? In the name of heaven, Kristie, don't take any more chances! Even suppose you were able to get a job on the staff, how long do you suppose it would be before you were spotted? Montevio himself may not visit the kitchen, but I'll guarantee that Señora de Mena does, and because she seemed friendly when she came here, don't imagine she'd accept you under her roof knowing you were there to harass her son.'

'Then how *can* I get to him?' Kristie demanded. 'Instead of telling me what I can't do, tell me something I can do! I have to get this interview somehow, Juan, and I let it slip away from me this morning because I was such a coward. Oh, why didn't I risk having to walk home and ask questions while I had the chance?'

'Because you were thinking sensibly for once,' Juan suggested, 'instead of trying to be something you're not.'

'And what is that supposed to mean?'

'That you try so hard to be the hardboiled reporter,' Juan said softly, 'when in fact you're a nice, pretty girl who wouldn't hurt a fly. Admit that Montevio frightens the life out of you, and you're halfway to being yourself; admit that he's more than you can cope with and it will be the most sensible thing you've ever said.'

Kristie was silent for several moments. It was rather disconcerting to have her innermost feelings so accurately spelled out, and she studied her hands as they lay on the table in front of her. Juan knew her almost too well, it seemed, and that in itself was discomfiting.

'You're making an awful lot of wild guesses,' she told him at last, then raised her eyes and deliberately challenged his assessment of her with a long hard look. 'I'll get that interview, you'll see.'

Juan looked at her, trying one last time to influence her. 'You're not going to take a bit of notice of me, are you?' he asked, and she shook her head regretfully.

'I need this wretched man's story, Juan.'

He sighed deeply and his dark eyes glowed with some inner warmth as he looked at her, his long hands placed together, palm to palm as if in prayer, the forefingers pulling down his lower lip. 'I don't pretend to understand you, *chica*,' he said, 'but you're much too hard to oppose. I know I ought to get really tough with you, but I simply can't.' His gaze lingered for a moment on her mouth, and he smiled. 'You're a dangerous woman, Kristie Roderigo,' he said softly, and for some reason she didn't understand, Kristie felt rather like crying.

Kristie had done far more shopping than she set out to do, but she seldom stuck rigidly to the list she wrote out for herself. Shopping was one thing that Juan hated doing, so she had thankfully escaped from his rather irritating vigilance for once and come alone. For a couple of days now he had stuck to her constantly, insisting that she wasn't safe to go out alone when she got herself involved with people like Montevio.

Kristie loved Seville. Even the constant noise of the traffic somehow failed to banish that lingering air of the romantic past. Elegant *plazas* and ancient houses recalled the days when lovesick gallants would come to woo the *señoritas* caged behind the barred windows; and secret, walled *patios* were still covered by awnings in summer and used as living-rooms by the families lucky enough to live there.

Rows of orange trees lined the streets and *plazas* and kept the worst of the summer heat at bay, but even so, after a couple of hours shopping Kristie was more than ready to seek out a small café she knew for refreshment and rest. It was the popular time for a mid-morning snack and most of the tables were taken, although there were one or two still available right at the back of the room.

It was while she was looking around that she heard her name, said very quietly and discreetly but from quite close by, and she turned swiftly, for the voice was unmistakable. Manuel Montevio was on his feet, standing by one of the small tables and very obviously about to ask her to join him, so that instinctively she sought for some excuse not to without even asking herself why.

He was wearing a hat which he raised just sufficiently far as good manners demanded then replaced, and dark glasses that gave him a disturbingly sinister air, and when she considered, Kristie wondered if she would have recognised him other than by his voice. 'Señorita Roderigo? Good morning, *señorita*, will you join me?'

There he stood a tall, commanding and vaguely menacing figure in a light fawn suit, and there was nothing she could do but accept his invitation. His table was partly in the sun, which could have accounted for him keeping his hat on, but Kristie suspected it was more likely to be with the object of concealing his conspicuous red-gold hair. A peasant woman in the foothills of the Sierra Morena might not recognise Montevio, but here in Seville there would be many who would.

'Are you quite recovered from your accident, *señorita*?'

His enquiry brought her swiftly back to earth, and she hastened to assure him, 'Oh yes, thank you, *señor*.'

'Please.' He indicated the chair next to his and the moment he had relieved her of her parcels and seen her seated, he called over a waiter, with that typical air of authority she had remarked on to Juan. 'What will you have, *señorita*?' he asked while the man hovered expectantly. 'Coffee or wine? And a pastry perhaps?'

'Coffee, please,' she said, 'nothing else.'

Even while the man was still within hearing, the eyes behind the dark glasses were taking note of the slender rounded shape shown off by her dress, and obviously appreciated what they saw. His mouth curved and relaxed into a smile. 'You surely don't need to study your diet, Señorita Roderigo, do you?' he asked, and for some reason she simply couldn't fathom, Kristie coloured furiously.

'I just like to play safe, that's all, *señor*.'

He removed his dark glasses, folded them carefully and placed them in the top pocket of his jacket, but never once took his eyes off her. 'And you blush,' he observed with a hint of amusement, 'how delightful!'

'*Señor*——'

She had been about to object, but he silenced her with a raised hand, and his moue of regret was quite unexpected, like his apology. 'I'm sorry, *señorita*, I don't mean to embarrass you, but it's rather unusual these days for a young woman to blush at a compliment, even in Spain.' He took a sip from his own cup, then leaned back, seemingly very much at ease and infinitely disturbing to Kristie's mind. 'Do you like Spain, Señorita Roderigo? You're not a native, are you, despite your name? It's your accent,' he explained when she looked up swiftly, 'it's very slight, but noticeable.'

Suddenly Kristie wondered if he had noticed it before, on other occasions, and hoped not. Juan had insisted that she had a slight accent when she was agitated, and there had never been an occasion yet when she had been in Manuel Montevio's company and not been agitated, but perhaps he hadn't noticed until now.

Once again she had been incredibly lucky, being thrown into his company, and this time Kristie did not intend to waste the opportunity if she could possibly help it. The only drawback was that she found him so disconcerting she needed to keep a firm hold on her self-possession, and she heaved an almost audible sigh of relief when the waiter brought her coffee.

'I'm not a native exactly,' she owned in answer to his query, 'but my father was Spanish, he died thirteen years ago. My mother is English—or more accurately Scottish, although she lives in England. I learnt Spanish from my father when I was little, and I come for a holiday with one or other of my relations most years.'

'Which accounts for the quality of your Spanish,' he said. 'As your mother's influence no doubt accounts for your blue eyes and beautiful skin.' It was impossible to remain unaffected by the deep, soft voice and almost slumbrous, heavy-lidded eyes that watched her so intently, and she once again coloured warmly. 'It's rather unusual to see blue eyes with black hair, but it's very lovely,' he went on. 'You're very fortunate, *señorita*.'

Slightly dazed by it all, Kristie shook her head. 'Back home it's often called Irish colouring. Black hair and blue eyes put in with a smutty finger, that's what they say.'

The colloquialism obviously puzzled him, for he half smiled, looking at her curiously and with his head tipped a little to one side. 'A—smutty finger?' he asked, and she laughed lightly, her own black-lashed eyes glowingly bright.

'Black eyelashes,' she explained, and he nodded.

'Ah, yes, I see the meaning.' He took another sip from his coffee and was obviously in no hurry to leave; and still that alarmingly disturbing gaze remained fixed on her. 'I'm surprised to see you alone, Señorita Roderigo; don't your family worry about you wandering about Seville on your own, knowing the reputation some of my country-men have?'

In fact Aunt Maria wasn't always happy about it and nor was Juan, who liked to accompany her whenever it was possible, but Kristie herself had no qualms at all and reckoned herself able to cope with any over-arduous Spanish male. 'My aunt fusses about it sometimes,' she told him with a smile, 'but we have the same kind of thing in England, *señor*, and I can cope.'

'I sincerely hope so!'

This could be the opening she had been looking for, Kristie thought. If he could ask questions of her she saw no reason why she couldn't do the same of him, and she leaned forward with her elbows on the table and one hand resting lightly at the side of her neck, the slight fluttering of her fingers being the only thing that betrayed her nervousness.

'Do you live in Seville, Señor Hernandez?' she asked, and noticed that he lowered his eyes to the cup he held between his hands before he answered her, although there was nothing in his reply to suggest evasiveness.

'On the outskirts, *señorita*, where it's both quieter and cooler.'

'Ah, then it's business that brings you into town! Do you have a business in Seville?'

It seemed to Kristie that he was some time answering, and his gaze lingered as if fascinated on the hand that hovered at the neck of her dress. 'I'm not in business, Señorita Roderigo,' he said eventually, 'in fact I'm writing a book.'

Kristie's look of surprise was no affectation, for although she remembered the van driver mentioning that Señora de Mena's son was a writer she had never seriously believed that Montevio had turned author. There was every reason why he would be writing a book, of course, for he must have had an interesting life on the motor-racing circuits, and he could write about it without giving away his whereabouts.

'That's interesting,' she said, and smiled, although it didn't quite reach her eyes because he had taken her by surprise, and her hand ran lightly down the neck of her dress, tracing the low neckline in a quite unconsciously provocative movement. 'Is it an autobiography, *señor*?'

It was when she noticed his expression that she realised it had been a mistake to suggest that, and his reply emphasised the fact. His eyes had narrowed slightly and there was perhaps a little less warmth in them, while the arrogant, back-tipped angle of his head was all too familiar. 'What makes you think anyone would be interested in reading *my* autobiography, Señorita Roderigo?' he asked, and even the quietness of his voice betrayed a change of mood.

'Oh, I don't know.' She shrugged, disturbingly aware as she did so that his gaze still lingered where her hand rested on the neck of her dress. When she laughed it had a curiously breathless sound, more like a gasp, and she shook her head. 'Doesn't everyone these days?' she asked. 'In England, anyway, it seems to me that every Tom, Dick and Harry is committing his life story to print.'

'Only those who have to some degree been in the public eye, surely?' he insisted, and again Kristie shrugged uneasily.

'I suppose so. Is your book fiction, then?'

'It's a crime story.'

'Oh, really? How far have you got? Is it almost finished?'

'Unfortunately no. Do you mind?' She shook her head automatically when he sought her permission before lighting a cigarette, and it wasn't until it was drawing to his satisfaction that he enlightened her further. 'At the moment I'm at a standstill because my regular secretary is away on holiday and the temporary replacement I was expecting to start work tomorrow morning has let me down at the last minute because of illness. It's annoying, because it means I'm held up for heaven knows how long.'

Kristie knew this was it, the moment she had been waiting for. A pulse throbbed hard at her temple and she almost shivered with excitement, for things really seemed to be going her way at last, although she would have to tread very carefully. If he had even the slightest suspicion of her she couldn't work it, and she would never have a chance like this again.

'It must be very frustrating for you,' she suggested, feeling her way carefully.

She had heard nothing about Marcos Francisco being taken ill, but he wasn't one of their friends that they saw very often and it was possible they wouldn't have heard. But sorry as she was for Marco, she couldn't help seeing it as a godsend for her. It was too soon yet to offer her own services, but the idea was firmly fixed in her mind and she waited eagerly for the right moment.

'Can't the agency find you another?' she asked, praying that they never would. 'He can't be the only secretary on their books, surely.'

Manuel removed a length of ash from his cigarette while she waited in breathless anxiety. 'It seems they haven't one with sufficient speed or stamina to suit me,' he said. 'Unfortunately really efficient secretaries aren't very easy to come by, and I need someone very fast as well as one prepared to work something more than normal office hours. It isn't the usual secretarial job by any means and very few are prepared to take it on.'

'So what can you do?'

He heaved his broad shoulders resignedly. 'Wait until I find someone suitable, if it's possible, if not——' Another shrug suggested he was far from happy about waiting, and Kristie saw her chance coming up at last.

Her heart was thudding hard and she had never felt more shiveringly nervous in her life before, but at the same time the prospect was exciting, she had to admit it. Working for Manuel Montevio would be no bed of roses, she could well imagine, but the opportunities of getting to know the man behind the enigma were surely boundless.

'I wonder——' She hesitated, while heavy-lidded eyes watched her with disconcerting steadiness, and she had the strangest feeling in the second before she spoke that he knew what she was going to say. She laughed, a small, unsteady sound that suggested she was reticent about what she was about to do, when in fact she felt wildly exhilarated at the nearness of success. 'I was just wondering if *I* could help,' she said, and the expression on his face did not change one iota.

'*You*, Señorita Roderigo?'

Something in the softness of his voice chased thrills up and down her spine, but she was too close now to think about anything else but clinching the agreement. 'I just thought,' she plunged on breathlessly, 'that as you're desperate for help, I might help you out.'

'You know shorthand and typing, *señorita*?'

Again the softness of his voice sent shivers through her, but she nodded unhesitatingly. 'I have very good speeds at both,' she assured him, 'and I'll quite willingly help you out until you find someone suitable. In fact I'd enjoy it, Señor Mo—Hernandez!'

That near slip could have been her undoing, but he appeared not to have noticed it. In fact it struck her as she watched him that he was taking it all very matter-of-factly when it must surely have come as a surprise to him. Very carefully he removed more ash from his cigarette and he didn't look up until it was done to his satisfaction.

'You're very kind, *señorita*,' he remarked coolly, 'but why should you be so willing to give up your holiday to help a stranger?'

That was a point, Kristie realised, and she sought desperately for a reason; then she smiled and shrugged lightly. 'But surely I owe you something for rescuing me the other day and then driving me home,' she told him, picking on the first thing that came to mind. 'If you hadn't been so insistent I might have fainted at the wheel and done both myself and Juan's car some permanent damage.'

'Juan is your cousin?'

She nodded, again aware of something in his manner that was not quite as she expected. He was leaning forward to use the ashtray again and for the moment his eyes were concealed by thick golden lashes as she watched the movement of long, strong fingers crushing out the smouldering tobacco, fascinated by the suggestion of violence without realising it. And when she answered him her voice was light and slightly unsteady.

'That's right, he owns the car I was driving. It isn't often I'm allowed to drive it myself, if I want to go anywhere Juan usually drives me.'

'Ah!' Almost as if it gave him some cause for satisfaction, she thought curiously. Then leaning back in his chair once more he fixed her with that steady and definitely disturbing gaze again, his eyes shadowed by the brim of his hat, darkly enigmatic. 'I'll accept your offer to help, Señorita Roderigo, as you've been kind enough to volunteer—unless of course you want to change your mind?'

'Oh no, definitely not!' That hint of challenge was unexpected and oddly disturbing somehow, but Kristie wasn't to be deterred at that point, and she shook her head. 'I'm only too pleased to be able to help in my turn.'

He had taken a small notebook from his pocket and sat with a pen poised over it, looking at her enquiringly. 'If you'll give me your address, Señorita Roderigo,' he said, 'I'll send a car to pick you up tomorrow morning. You can begin in the morning?' he insisted, and Kristie nodded a little dazedly.

It was all going rather fast, and she only just stopped herself from telling him that she knew where to go and that Juan would run her out to the Villa de los Naranjos. Instead she very reluctantly gave him Aunt Maria's address and hoped she wouldn't live to regret it, while he very carefully made a note of it in his little book. When he had finished he looked across at her again and a faint smile touched the corners of his mouth but did not, she noted uneasily, show in his eyes.

'How fortunate we met, Señorita Roderigo,' he said, and Kristie almost laughed aloud.

How could she have dreamed such an opportunity would come her way? She could scarcely wait to tell Juan what she had achieved simply by making the most of her chances and proving herself a good journalist. 'Very fortunate,' she agreed.

CHAPTER FOUR

KRISTIE not only felt excited at the prospect ahead of her, she also felt nervous, although she preferred not to admit it even to herself. The following morning as she got herself ready, she consoled herself with the thought that nothing very awful could happen to her with Señora de Mena in the same house. The worst that Manuel could do if he should happen to discover who she was would be to forcibly evict her as he had done on the last occasion.

It had been a little difficult explaining it to Aunt Maria, but eventually she had accepted the story that Kristie had offered to help out an author she had met because his secretary had gone sick. The fact that her aunt had commended her for her thoughtfulness had made her feel a bit guilty about deceiving her, but Kristie told herself it was all in a good cause.

Juan, on the other hand, with knowledge of the true situation, was much more unhappy about it and brooded on possible consequences while he did his best to make her change her mind. 'Don't go, *chica*,' he pleaded. 'I don't like it, I don't like it at all.'

'But it's too good an opportunity to miss,' Kristie argued. 'I couldn't believe my luck when he said Marcos was sick and couldn't start tomorrow, although I'm sorry about Marcos naturally.'

'That's one of the things I'm not happy about,' Juan told her, and she looked at him and frowned. 'There's nothing wrong with Marcos,' he went on. 'I saw him last night in the café and he was as fit as ever I've seen him, so why should Montevio lie about it?'

'I don't know!' She shrugged off the recollection of Manuel's almost coolly matter-of-fact acceptance of her offer, and shook her head. 'Maybe he's found out that Marcos isn't as efficient as he'd been led to believe,' she

suggested, but Juan was shaking his head and the way he
pursed his lower lip showed how unlikely he thought it.

'More likely he decided he'd rather have a pretty girl
working for him-instead of a man,' he said. 'Or has it
occurred to you that he might realise who you are,
Kristie?'

'No, definitely not!' She shook her head firmly. 'I suppose your first suggestion is a possibility, but the second—
definitely not. Can you honestly see him letting me into
his home when he knows I'm after an interview with him,
Juan?'

But he still wasn't happy about her going, and he sat
with his chin on one hand, the elbow resting on the table
in front of him and gazing broodingly across at her.
Because she had to make a very early start they had eaten
breakfast much earlier than usual, and they now sat together on the *patio*, waiting for the promised car to call
for her.

'Oh, don't worry about it!' Kristie leaned across and
squeezed his hand. 'There's a perfectly rational explanation for it, I'm sure, and whatever reason Montevio had
for making up that story about Marco being ill, I can't
let this chance pass, Juan—you must see that.'

'I see you heading for a whole lot of trouble,' he prophesied gloomily, and because she was rather less confident than she appeared, Kristie laughed and shook her
head at him.

'You're a gloomy old pessimist,' she told him. 'Why
should anything go wrong?'

'It will,' Juan promised grimly. 'For one thing, even if
he doesn't already know who you are, he's going to know
soon enough when you try to interview him, and you know
what that will mean.'

'At worst it means I shall have to walk home,' she told
him with a wry smile, 'and I've done that before; don't
worry, Juan.'

'How can I help it?' Juan demanded and, taking both
her hands in his, he looked at her with dark anxious eyes
that did disturbing things to her conscience. 'You don't

know what might happen, Kristie, and Señora de Mena is going to be firmly on the side of her son if it comes to a showdown. She isn't going to do anything to help you prod him into the limelight again.'

'I'll be careful, I promise.'

She half turned her head as Juan did, listening to a car pulling up in the street just outside the *patio* gate, and her heart was thudding hard as she got to her feet. Juan had put too many doubts into her mind, and she was determined not to be put off, so she deliberately put on a big, bright smile as she called out to her aunt.

'Wish me luck, dear Juan,' she whispered, and bent to kiss him lightly beside his mouth.

'I just wish I could talk you out of going!' Juan declared huskily, and with a hand on each of her arms he pulled her down towards him, his mouth firm and hard on hers for a moment before he let her go. 'Good luck, my pigeon, and if anything happens to you I'll personally make sure that Montevio never makes a pass at another girl as long as he lives!'

His passionate fierceness was something new to her, and she felt curiously unsteady on her legs as she walked quickly along the path, knowing that he watched her every step of the way. She loved him for his concern, but she wished he had been more encouraging, for she already knew just how much she had taken on.

The limousine that awaited her could have been the same one that had collected Señora de Mena after her visit that day, and there was a liveried chauffeur to open the door for her too. He saw her into the back seat, then looked around him curiously. 'You have no more baggage, *señorita*?' he asked, and Kristie looked puzzled as she shook her head.

'Just my handbag,' she told him.

The man hesitated for a moment, then shrugged and closed the door after her. Whatever misapprehension he had been labouring under he was soon convinced, and minutes later they were driving along the quiet tree-lined streets that were almost deserted at that time of day.

Kristie's heart was thudding hard and her cheeks had a faint flush of anticipation as she sat back in comfort feeling just a little bit smug. This was the moment she had been waiting for ever since she first learned that Manuel Montevio was in Seville; she was on her way to his home and at his invitation this time. The fact that she had volunteered was neither here nor there, he had accepted her offer and she had her best opportunity yet of getting near to him.

She was only vaguely aware of the eyes that glanced at her every so often via the driving mirror, and it was some time before she realised that the car had turned north out of Seville instead of west on to the San Pedro road. Frowning curiously, she leaned forward in her seat to question the chauffeur.

'Where are you taking me?' she asked. 'This isn't the way to the Villa de los Naranjos.'

'That's right, *señorita*, we're going to the castle.'

The man's eyes were watching her again via the mirror and she could have sworn he looked faintly amused. She could not forget all those forebodings of Juan's and her pulse was throbbing hard at her temple, making it very hard to think clearly. It was too soon, and she was too unprepared for things to start going wrong already.

'The castle?' she asked. 'What castle? You are from Señor Hernandez, aren't you?'

'Yes, of course, *señorita*, and I was told to take you to the castle.'

He checked following traffic, then turned off the main road on to a steeper and much narrower one that was suddenly startlingly familiar. It was on this same road that she had almost collided with Manuel Montevio when she was driving Juan's car, and when she realised it apprehension began to outweigh excitement and satisfaction. She recalled again the easy, almost matter-of-fact acceptance of her offer to help and suspicion gnawed at her confidence as she sat on the very edge of her seat with her fingers gripping the back of the chauffeur's seat.

'You haven't answered me,' she insisted in a raggedly

uncertain voice. 'What castle is it you're taking me to, and why aren't we going to the Villa de los Naranjos?'

'It's the Castillo Cuchicheo, *señorita*, where Señor Hernandez works.'

'Oh, I see.' She had to admit that a castle in the mountains was probably an ideal place for an author to work, but they seemed to have come an awful long way and they were still travelling. 'How far is this Castillo Cuchicheo?' she asked.

'Another thirty kilometres, *señorita*; it's right up in the mountains.'

He was watching her via the mirror and he saw her eyes widen and her mouth open in blank surprise. 'Thir—thirty kilometres?'

'That's right, *señorita*.'

It dawned on her at last why the man had expected to see her with more than just a handbag, but it made her more than ever uneasy about Manuel's motive for accepting her offer to help. He had said nothing about the post being a live-in one, but, while it made sense that it would be in the circumstances, it didn't fit in with her conception of Manuel Montevio that he would have been too absentminded to mention it.

She tried not to sound too surprised, but doubted if she fooled the man, who glanced at her once more with a hint of speculation in his eyes. 'Am I expected to live in?'

'I assume so, *señorita*. The *señor*'s secretary has always been a resident one. He'd find it too distracting to have someone coming and going every day, then there's the inconvenient hours, of course.'

'I didn't realise that,' Kristie said. 'I thought I'd be working at the villa.' She met his eyes briefly and thought she detected a hint of sympathy. 'It's very awkward, I haven't anything with me except a handbag.'

'Leave it all to the *señor* to arrange,' the man told her encouragingly. 'He's a real gentleman, *señorita*, you'll have nothing to worry about up there, although I've never known him have a lady secretary before.' He gave her a brief wink via the mirror and smiled. 'Maybe he likes the idea of a pretty girl for a change, eh?'

Just what Juan had suggested, Kristie remembered, and told herself that if it was true she wasn't entirely averse to the idea as long as things didn't get too much out of hand. 'I volunteered,' she told the man. 'I heard the temporary secretary was taken ill and offered to take his place.'

Only Marco wasn't taken ill, according to Juan. The chauffeur howeyer, obviously saw no reason for concern, and he seemed an ordinary and decent enough sort of man. 'Well, it'll make a nice change,' he said. 'And don't worry about your things, *señorita*, he'll arrange something. I'll probably be sent back to Seville to get something for you—don't worry.'

Maybe she was being too suspicious, Kristie thought; it was Juan's fault for being such a pessimist. In fact she was doing exactly what she had been trying to do ever since she heard about Montevio being on hand, and she should make the most of it. Certainly there was nothing to complain of in the scenery this far up in the mountains, although it seemed very empty and lonely.

It was the first time she had been this far up into the Sierra Morena and the river that normally ran virtually alongside the road she was driving on was now no more than a thin thread of silver way below. They were surrounded by miles of rugged peaks clothed in low-growing maquis, and she couldn't help but be impressed by the idea of working in a castle.

They took a sharp turn suddenly and she caught her breath when they seemed to hang for a heart-stopping moment on the very edge of a deep chasm. With practised aplomb the driver took them round smoothly, and in silence pointed to a castle perched high up and right at the summit of the chasm wall, so that it seemed to have been built of the same rock as it loomed upward into the hot blue sky.

It was an old Moorish castle and the views from its many windows must have been breathtaking. It had the rugged impression of power and beauty combined that only Spain could offer, and it stirred her senses un-

expectedly. 'Castillo Cuchicheo?' she asked, and the man
nodded. 'It—it's very isolated.'

'The *señor* likes solitude, especially when he's working,'
he said, and gave her a swift grin. 'I hope you do too,
señorita!'

Kristie was not prepared to commit herself. The castle
was isolated, for there was no other habitation in sight,
only miles of rolling mountain scenery and a searingly
blue sky. An eyrie in the wilderness and alarmingly far
from home. Her attention was distracted again when the
car was turned off the road and on to an even narrower
one that led on over what had almost certainly been a
drawbridge once, then into a shadowed courtyard by way
of a low stone archway.

The Moorish origins of the castle were evident in the
colonnades of lacy stone arches that surrounded the
courtyard, and the tiled courtyard itself with its lion fountain. It was beautiful, yet curiously still and lifeless, and
she realised it was because there was no water running
through the fountain. In fact the whole place had an air of
stillness, as if it waited for something or someone, and the
rather fanciful thought made her shiver for a moment.

As she stepped out of the car she was struck by a curious
low, whispering sound that sounded like distant, muffled
voices, and startled by the eeriness of it, she turned and
looked at the chauffeur for enlightenment. He was smiling
and shaking his head. 'You'll get used to it, *señorita*,' he
told her. 'It's just the wind on the mountain echoing in
the chasm.'

'It's spooky.' She hastily suppressed another shiver, then
nodded understanding as the man led her in under the
tracery of stone arches to a half-open door. 'Of course,
that's why it's called the Whispering Castle, I suppose.'

'That's right, *señorita*.'

He opened a huge, nail-studded black door and ushered
her into the biggest hall Kristie had ever seen. It was very
sparsely furnished, yet did not suggest poverty or neglect,
and the silence was almost overpowering except for that
persistent whisper of sound as the mountain wind swept

across that huge chasm and through the tracery of stone-work.

The floor was tiled with beautiful Moorish *azulejos* that echoed their footsteps as they walked, and above her a high ceiling seemed to soar to infinity where shadows hinted at dark, gilded beams. A curved staircase rose in a sweeping line of intricately carved balusters, gilded and gleaming, the stone treads worn into hollows with genera-tions of feet, making a curious design of their own. It was impressive, despite the sparseness of the furnishing, and Kristie was momentarily overwhelmed by it.

She came swiftly back to earth when she realised an elderly man had emerged from a room on the far side and was coming towards them, treading soft-footed in felt slip-pers and watching them all the time with the blackest eyes Kristie had ever seen. He didn't speak, but merely inclined his head in Kristie's direction, then used his hands to make swift, unintelligible signs to the chauffeur, who seemed to have no difficulty understanding them.

'The *señorita* has no luggage,' he informed the man, and shrugged his shoulders in a way that absolved him from blame. 'Apparently she was not told to bring anything, so I'd better wait and see if I have to fetch some things for her.'

The older man nodded, then by a gesture of one hand invited her to follow him. Something about the situation still did not seem right, but not for anything was Kristie going to make waves at this point, so she obediently followed her guide across the hall, stepping past him with a murmur of thanks when he opened a door and stood back to allow her in ahead of him.

It was an impressive room, though not as vast as the hall, and in here at least there was comfort and luxury with carpeted floor and gleaming dark furniture. There was a vast window to one side that gave an awe-inspiring view of the chasm above which the castle was built, and as she was shown in, Manuel Montevio turned from con-templating it and looked at her instead.

He had discarded his jacket which was draped over the

back of a chair, and in shirt sleeves he was a disturbingly earthy figure, a fact that struck her anew when she saw him. His hands were clasped behind him and served to stress the muscular power of his arms, and through the thin cream shirt she was again struck by the impression of golden flesh and a hint of thick light hair at the base of the opening. The room had the bright reflection of sunlight from outside and it seemed to make his red-gold hair gleam like bronze, reminding her of his famous soubriquet. He was every inch the Golden Spaniard, and Kristie found him alarmingly affecting as they stood looking at one another for a moment.

He didn't approach her, but stayed where he was in the great curve of the window, with the mountains behind him and his face slightly shadowed; dark and enigmatic. 'Good morning, Señorita Roderigo.' The snick of the door closing behind her made her swing round swiftly, and when she looked back he was regarding her with raised brows. 'Please don't let José make you nervous, he's perfectly normal, except that he's mute.'

'Oh, he doesn't make me nervous!' She denied it hastily, and fought hard to steady her voice as she went on. 'It's just that—this isn't exactly what I was expecting, Señor Hernandez.'

'In what way, *señorita*?'

The deep cool voice seemed somehow to be mocking her, and yet there was nothing else to suggest he was being anything other than polite over a genuine confusion. She didn't want to start by complaining about the situation she was expected to work in, and yet she couldn't just appear to accept it or he would surely be suspicious.

'Well, naturally I didn't expect to travel nearly seventy kilometres to work, *señor*, and your chauffeur tells me that your regular secretary lives in. You didn't say anything to me about that.'

His eyes surveyed her for a moment between thick golden lashes, and his lower lip was thrust out slightly, as if he gave the situation some consideration before he replied. 'Would you have come if I had, Señorita

Roderigo?' he asked, and something in the softness of his voice slid like an icy finger along Kristie's spine.

She supposed she would have come, whatever the situation, as long as she could gain his confidence and get close enough to him to press home her advantage when the opportunity arose, but she could hardly tell him so. Instead she shook her head slowly, more wary than she had ever been with anyone in her life before.

'I don't suppose so,' she admitted, and quickly averted her own eyes when she realised he was still watching her with that unnervingly steady gaze.

'Do you wish to change your mind and leave again?' That sounded alarmingly like a challenge to Kristie, and she didn't know how she was expected to reply. 'You have only to say,' he went on, 'and you can be driven back to Seville.'

How could she let it slip through her fingers now that she had come so far? Kristie squirmed inwardly at the situation he had put her into, and yet she had no real reason to believe he had done other than make a genuine mistake by not mentioning the fact of her living in. She couldn't let it go, not after all the high hopes she had had of being his secretary, for however short a time, and she sought wildly for a way to accept without making it appear she was over-eager.

'I—I did promise I'd help out,' she reminded him. 'It isn't for very long, Señor Hernandez, and if—if you'll let me take the car back to Seville I can explain to my aunt and collect some things——'

The impatient clicking of his tongue cut her short, and Kristie looked at him warily. 'I've lost enough time already, Señorita Roderigo, with the temporary man not turning up, it would suit me much better if you write your aunt a note, asking her to pack what you need, and Esteban will take it to her and bring your things back.'

'Couldn't I telephone her instead?' Kristie ventured, and she noticed that he smiled faintly as he shook his head.

'There's no telephone here, *señorita*; the castle is completely isolated because it suits me that way when I'm working.'

'Oh, I see.' It was as if another door had slammed on her, and in Kristie's imagination she was getting in deeper and deeper without any real idea of what she was getting into. The one thought that consoled her was that there was sure to be a housekeeper, and the presence of another woman was always reassuring. She smiled, a very small and uncertain smile but enough to convince him, she hoped. 'Well, in that case I'd better write a note to Aunt Maria as you said, and let her know what's going on— and just hope she isn't too shocked at the idea of me living in!'

For a moment his eyes held hers steadily, then a hint of smile touched his mouth, his voice deep and smooth and far from reassuring despite the words. 'You may assure your aunt that she had nothing at all to worry about,' he told her. 'You'll be quite safe, *señorita*.'

As he steered her across to a small desk in one corner of the room, Kristie could only pray he was right. There was a lot about the situation that made her uneasy, and it went without saying that Juan's reaction would be something much more forceful. She only hoped he wouldn't do anything to spoil the opportunity she was taking so many chances for; however right he might be about Manuel Montevio being more dangerous than she realised, she had gone too far now to back off.

It seemed to Kristie that they had been working non-stop for the whole day, and it was in fact well over four hours since Manuel Montevio began dictating. They had worked through without the customary mid-morning break and, having had a very early breakfast, Kristie found the smell of cooking that occasionally wafted in to them taunting her empty stomach unmercifully.

Manuel, on the other hand, showed no sign of flagging, and he had had nothing more to keep him going than an occasional sip from a glass to ease his dry throat. He had not even glanced at his wristwatch as Kristie had done several times during the last hour; nor had he lied when he said he needed someone fast, for it had taken all Kristie's skill to keep up with him, and after getting on for five hours' concentrated effort she realised that she would soon have to call halt if he didn't.

Her chance came when he at last finished dictating, and suggested she type out what they had done so far. Kristie looked across at him and ventured a half-smile, even though he didn't look up. 'Shan't we be taking a break soon?' she asked, and his expression made it clear that the idea had not even occurred to him.

'A break?' he echoed, frowning over it, then he glanced briefly at his watch. 'I hope you aren't one of those people who expect to work by the clock and take breaks every five minutes,' he said. 'The hours I work are long and irregular, Señorita Roderigo, and anyone who keeps one eye on the clock is no use to me!'

Her stomach rolling, Kristie glared at him. She was tired and hungry, and she could have reminded him that she was doing him a favour by being there at all, but she could see that that would probably be an end of her tenuous hold on the post of secretary. So instead of making an issue of it, she kept a firm hold on her temper, and nodded, biting hard on her lip when another delicious waft invaded the room briefly.

'No, of course not,' she murmured.

He didn't even offer an apology, but bent his head over a pile of notes on his desk and proceeded to ignore her, while Kristie gave her stomach a surreptitious rub before rolling the first sheet into her typewriter. It was another hour before she made another attempt to call a halt, and by then she was so ravenously hungry that the smell of cooking was sheer torture.

It was after three-thirty and, even though she was familiar with the lateness of Spanish mealtimes, she knew that this had gone beyond the bounds of reason. However hard he meant to work her, she couldn't go much longer without something to eat, and she meant to tell him so, whatever the outcome. Carefully placing the last sheet she had typed on top of the pile, she looked across at him and took a deep breath.

'Señor Hernandez,' she announced firmly, 'I'm not doing any more work until I've had something to eat.'

He sat for a moment looking across at her, his light brows drawn above glittering amber eyes, then he got to his feet and came slowly over to her, so that Kristie's heart began a wildly irregular beat that made it hard to think clearly. 'Is it your usual practice, announcing your intention to stop work?' he asked, and leaned with both hands on her desk, bringing his face disconcertingly close. 'Is this the way you normally behave towards your employer, Señorita Roderigo? Or do you feel you have more privileges in your present situation?'

'Privileges!' It was much too disturbing, having him looming over her, so she got to her feet, brushing one hand through the hair on her forehead in a gesture that was unconsciously defiant. 'I volunteered to act as temporary secretary, Señor Hernandez, and so far I've more reason to regret it than to feel I'm privileged! No employer has ever kept me working for five and half solid hours before without a break, and as I had my breakfast just after seven this morning you don't have to be told how hungry I am!'

'I've worked the same hours.'

'From choice!' She took heed of a warning bell that reminded her she could so easily lose her hard-won advantage if she said too much, but even so she wasn't going to let him walk roughshod all over her. 'As the post is a live-in one,' she went on, 'I presume I get fed.'

'It's customary.'

'But *when*?' Kristie demanded exasperatedly. It appalled her to realise that she was actually close to tears; hunger and hours of unrelieved concentration were taking their toll of her self-possession. 'When I volunteered to help,' she told him desperately, 'I didn't anticipate you'd be starving me!'

'Well, of course I won't,' Manuel assured her smoothly, 'it wouldn't be practical.'

His coolness staggered her, and anger was rapidly beginning to overtake caution. 'Oh, good!' She saw her sarcasm fall on stony ground. 'And *where* do I eat, when I do? In the kitchen among the pots and pans perhaps?'

He looked as if he was actually considering it, and she found it hard to believe as she stared at the harsh lines of his face and gleaming eyes. 'I think not,' he decided. 'José would find it embarrassing having you in the kitchen.'

'Then where?'

He looked as if he would like to have insisted on carrying on with work, but perhaps the unmistakable look in her eyes warned him not to push her too far. 'This way,' he said, and Kristie hastened after him when he went striding off out of the room and into the hall. The odours from the kitchen were even stronger as they crossed the hall, and as he led the way to another room almost opposite, Kristie was almost running to keep up with him, her stomach clamouring for satisfaction.

This room was small, completely different from the one they had just left; more cosy in a way that was unexpected somehow in the vast silence of the castle. It was white-walled and carpeted, and titillatingly full of delicious smells, so that she was already feeling more amiable towards him when he saw her seated before taking his own place at the head of the table.

The long dark table looked as ancient as the castle itself, and was set for two with rich silver and dazzling white linen, making it evident that she had never been intended to eat in the kitchen. There was a curious sense of satisfaction in sharing a meal with him too, for their chairs were set intimately side by side, instead of one at each end.

Manuel said little, but for the moment that was the way Kristie preferred it, for at the moment the need to satisfy her appetite was of first importance. Even so she found it alarmingly disturbing being seated next to him, and there was a light, fluttering beat to her pulse as they sat waiting for their meal to be served to them.

Her eyes were drawn irresistibly to the physical aspects

of him with an intensity as never before. To the strong
hands and bare brown arms, and a glimpse of broad chest
at the open front of his shirt; the column of throat with its
steadily beating pulse, and the regular rise and fall of his
breathing. She had never before been so physically aware
of a man; of his undeniable sensuality, and the sheer
earthy maleness of him, and her own pulse was more rapid
because of it.

She snatched herself quickly back to earth when another door opened on the far side of the room to admit
the short stocky figure of José, the mute manservant, now
smartly turned out in a short white jacket. It would be
difficult, Kristie surmised, to get staff who were willing to
work in such isolated surroundings, so perhaps there was
only José and his wife to act as cook-housekeeper and
general factotum.

The food was excellent, and the baked fish that was
their first course was eaten in complete silence, both of
them it seemed too hungry to indulge in conversation. It
was only when José brought in a dish of stewed chicken
and served them both before discreetly withdrawing that
Kristie passed a remark about the excellence of the meal.

'José's wife must be worth her weight in gold,' she
observed, 'when she can cook like this.'

She swallowed a fragrant mouthful of chicken before
she looked at him, sensing something significant in his
silence. Manuel finished his own mouthful, then met her
eyes steadily and with the disturbing intensity that was
becoming increasingly familiar. 'José isn't married,
Señorita Roderigo,' he told her. 'He cooked the meal
himself, just as he does everything else; he's the only staff
I have here.'

Kristie stared at him and her heart was pounding hard.
'Not— not even a housekeeper?' she asked in a shaky
whisper, and Manuel continued with his meal as if unaware of her reaction.

'No!'

'But— the chauffeur who brought me here?'

'Esteban?' He looked up briefly, as if the question surprised him, then once more got on with his meal. 'He drove back to Seville and brought back your belongings—they're in your room, incidentally—and then he returned to Seville. I don't keep a car here when I'm working, I live in complete isolation as far as it's practicable. No one calls again now until the car comes at the week's end—no one.'

There was nothing untoward about it at all, Kristie told herself; it was quite logical that he would ensure complete isolation if that was the way he worked best. In normal circumstances, when his regular male secretary was there, the situation would be perfectly commonplace; it was only her own presence that made it different.

For a second or two he relinquished his interest in his meal, and leaned towards her slightly, so close that she could discern a web of fine lines at the corner of each eye. 'I hope you're not nervous, Señorita Roderigo,' he said in a shiveringly soft voice.

Kristie fought hard against the idea that he was deliberately trying to alarm her, and instead kept her mind on less dangerous matters. 'That day I almost collided with you, you were coming from here,' she guessed, and he agreed unhesitatingly, still carrying on with his meal while she scarcely touched hers.

'That was a rare occasion,' he assured her, 'and not something that's likely to happen during your stay, señorita. The car does only the two trips a week normally; to bring me here and to fetch me back. This week Esteban drove me up last night because I wanted to go through my notes before we started this morning, but this week is somewhat—different.'

'Yet knowing what the situation was here,' Kristie accused in a flat little voice, 'you didn't hesitate to have me brought here.'

Manuel picked up his wine glass and for a moment regarded her over its rim, then he moved his gaze slowly over her flushed face to the tremulous fullness of her mouth and on to the open neck of her dress, where a shadowy curve hinted at the more full curves below and trembled with the quickness of her breathing.

Normally she was perfectly capable of handling any situation involving a man, but this was no ordinary man, and she felt alarmingly out of her depth. The delicious smell of the chicken stew no longer tempted her, and where before she had been ravenously hungry, she now no longer had any interest in food.

'Don't you like the chicken?' Manuel asked with apparent concern. 'José will be very disappointed if you don't eat it.'

'Oh—oh yes, it's very good.'

It was as much as she could do to keep up an appearance of normality when she believed less and less that the situation was a normal one, and she was much too anxious to know what he was going to say or do next to eat anything. If only she could be sure just why he was behaving as he was, it might be easier to anticipate his next move.

'You insisted you were too hungry to go on working,' he reminded her, and to Kristie the gleam in his eyes looked disturbingly malicious. 'Have you suddenly lost your appetite, Señorita Roderigo?'

Her heart thudding uneasily, Kristie put down her knife and fork and clenched her hands into tight fists either side of her plate, her tongue flicking anxiously over her lips. 'You must know I'm not very happy about this—this situation, Señor Hernandez,' she said huskily. 'I came here in good faith——'

'Did you?'

She avoided the challenge in his eyes warily, and shook her head. 'I came to help out because——'

'You came for the same reason that you twice invaded the privacy of my home!' Manuel interrupted harshly, and Kristie caught her breath, faced with the truth at last. 'You're here because you couldn't resist taking advantage of an opportunity that must have seemed heaven-sent to a prying reporter on the scent of a story! Whatever kind of man I'm supposed to be, do you think I'd bring a nice, ordinary girl into a situation like this?'

'I'm an ordinary girl,' Kristie insisted. 'I just happen to

have a job you don't approve of!'

'You're a cheat and a liar!'

'And you're not?' All the passion of her Spanish blood fired her as she glared at him, between desperation and regret. 'You lied about Marcos Francisco being ill—he *isn't* ill, Juan saw him in town last night.'

'You knew that, but you still came!' His steady look scorned her. 'Surely a nice ordinary girl, such as you claim to be, would have stayed home rather than come to a strange place to a man she barely knew. She certainly wouldn't have jumped in without hesitation because she was determined to get her own way whatever she had to do to achieve it!'

It was the harder to take because so much of what he said was true, but to Kristie it was as if the sky had suddenly fallen in, and his revenge was so much more harsh than she had anticipated. Still too confused to recognise that the pretence was over, she spoke in a small and very unsteady voice, using the name she had schooled herself to call him.

'Señor Hernandez——'

'Since you know my name you might as well use it,' he told her roughly. 'Unlike you, I don't really enjoy masquerading! Tell me, which one is really you? The brassy blonde at my gates, or the swooning brunette? Myself, I found the brunette much more attractive!'

He startled her so much when he grasped a handful of her hair that Kristie cried out, putting her hands up to relieve the effect of the savage tug he gave it before letting go. He hurt her, and as she scrambled to her feet she did so in such haste that she almost fell over, and her eyes were bright and sparkling with mingled anger and reproach as she stood with one hand to her tingling scalp.

When he followed her example and got to his feet, she automatically backed away, only to be brought up short by the wall behind her, and he looked so gloweringly fierce as he towered over her that fear fluttered chillingly in her stomach for a moment. Staring at him, she spread her hands against the wall and wondered what chance she stood if she turned and ran.

'You never will understand,' she told him in a breathlessly small voice. 'What I did was to try and get a story; I was doing what I'm paid for. What you did was deliberately malicious; you told me Marcos was sick just so that——'

'Knowing you wouldn't be able to resist volunteering,' Manuel finished for her, and his eyes glittered mockingly as he watched her. 'Once I realised who you were I set out to teach you a lesson, my dear *señorita*. Your friend will be none the worse off for being told his services were not required after all; it will be worth paying him for nothing to see how you cope. And, as you've remarked on several occasions today, you *did* volunteer.'

'I didn't anticipate walking into a trap!'

He stood too close for comfort and his eyes gleamed at her, looking like molten gold between their thick lashes. 'You thought you had the better of me and you don't like having the tables turned! Is your name Roderigo, by the way, or is that simply another masquerade?'

'No, it's my own name!'

'Ah, so you really are half Spanish; at least there's something about you that's genuine!'

Her confidence seemed to have fled for the moment as she leaned back against the wall feeling slightly sick with the bitterness of disappointment and wondering what might happen next. Her head was spinning, for she had no idea what to do, or even if she could do anything to extricate herself. If he had told the truth there was no one else in the castle but the two of them and the mute man-servant, José, and that was the most disturbing factor of all at the moment.

'What—what are you going to do?' she asked, and the sudden swift and savage look that swept over her brought bright hot colour to her cheeks.

'Not what you might have in mind,' Manuel told her in a voice that shrivelled the last of her confidence. 'You came here to work, ostensibly, and I'm going to see that you do just that, Señorita Roderigo; I'm going to see that you work until you drop! You've never worked so hard as you're going to for the next week, my dear *señorita*, believe me!'

Kristie ran a hasty tongue over her lips, a small, anxious gesture that she realised, too late, must have given him some satisfaction. Then she shook her head. 'You can't——' she began, then shook her head because she knew how wrong she was.

'You doubt it?' Manuel challenged harshly. 'If you're still of a mind to write about me when you leave here there'll be nothing I can do to prevent you, but at least some of what you write will have the virtue of truth. Let us hope, however, by the time I've finished with you you won't feel so enthusiastic about writing anything!'

To Kristie, who had expected she would be sent packing without hesitation, having been firmly put in her place, the plan he proposed was a stunning alternative, and she wasn't sure that departure wouldn't have been the lesser of two evils. What he had in mind for her sounded formidable and she had no doubt that he intended to do exactly as he threatened.

Still clinging to what little self-possession she had left, she lifted her head and looked directly at him, determined not to let him see her defeated. 'I'll work,' she told him huskily. 'It's what I came to do.'

'Oh, indeed you will,' Manuel assured her with dangerous softness. 'You'll be surprised just how hard you *can* work, Señorita Roderigo!'

CHAPTER FIVE

DINNER the night before had been something of an ordeal, but still Kristie had managed to do justice to José's excellent cooking. The meal had been fairly late too, although Manuel had decided to call it a day just after seven o'clock, having worked her harder than she ever had before. If he intended keeping up that pace, she thought, she wasn't sure she could last the week, which was presumably as long as he intended keeping her there.

Her room was in keeping with what a castle bedroom should be, in her opinion, although its lack of femininity suggested it was normally used by Manuel's resident male secretary. If she had a fault to find with it it was that it was far too big, but it was cool and comfortable, and she had slept well enough.

She had assumed that breakfast would be the usual Spanish one of rolls with butter and jam or honey, and she wasn't disappointed when she came down fairly late the following morning. Manuel was already part way through his meal, and he very pointedly looked at his wristwatch when she came in. 'Good morning, Señorita Roderigo.'

Somehow the normality of the greeting struck a wrong note, and Kristie laughed shortly as she sat down in the place José had set for her, right next to Manuel at the top of the table. 'How can you sound so—so ordinary?' she demanded, not bothering to return his greeting.

'Courtesy, *señorita*,' he replied smoothly. 'Perhaps it isn't a commodity you're very familiar with.'

'I'd hardly call it courtesy when you're talking about working me like a slave after I've offered to help out,' Kristie argued. 'I'd call it sheer ingratitude!'

'If your motive really had been as generous as you're trying to make it sound, I'd have to agree,' Manuel said in the same cool voice, 'but in the circumstances I'd call it a just and practical reaction. You wanted to come here and I needed a secretary, this way we both get what we want, although perhaps not quite in the way you'd envisaged. It is to all intents a very practical form of revenge, you'll have to agree.'

'I find it hard to agree with anything you say or do,' Kristie told him, and bit with savage satisfaction into a bread roll. 'I wouldn't even sit at the same table with you, but having been warned of what's in store for me and not knowing when I'll get another meal, I need to have a good breakfast!' It annoyed her that he didn't even look up, but got on with his own meal, and after a moment or two she looked at him obliquely from the corner of her eye, giving voice to something that had been puzzling her ever since the previous day. 'I still don't know how you got on to me,' she said, and when he looked up at last she could see quite clearly that the anger of yesterday still lurked in his eyes, and his mouth was a hard, firm line.

'You will insist on taking me for a fool,' he said, and the resentment he felt made his voice as harsh as his frown.

Startled that he should even think it, Kristie looked at him and shook her head. 'I've never done anything of the kind,' she insisted firmly, but he seemed not to have heard her, frowning instead over what he himself was saying, as if he found it hard to believe.

'Only once did you fool me completely, and that was when we almost collided on the mountain road.' He met her wavering gaze with a burning resentment, and Kristie guessed that he condemned himself almost as harshly as he did her. 'I had no idea on that occasion that you were anything other than a very lovely girl, more than ordinarily attractive, and in need of my help. Not even when I invited you to join me in the café a few days later did it occur to me that you were anything other than what you appeared—not in the first few moments, that is.'

And he had been bitterly disillusioned, Kristie realised,

and recognised her own regret. Her pulse was hammering hard as she looked at the dark enigma of his face, for he had all but admitted that he found her attractive on that first occasion, when they had almost collided on the road, and his disillusionment must have been all the more bitter when he learned who she really was.

'Once it began to dawn on me how I'd been fooled,' Manuel went on in the same harshly condemning voice, 'I began to see how even the so-called accident on the road had been just another trick. Although even now I can't imagine why you didn't take advantage of the drive back to Seville to get your wretched interview—or at least try to.'

'Because it wasn't a trick,' Kristie insisted, and it seemed suddenly very important to convince him of that. 'How could I possibly have known I'd meet you on that road? And I didn't even know this castle existed, let alone that you owned it—how could I?'

Manuel curled his lip and she found it very hard to meet his eyes, for they condemned her out of hand for every attempt she had made to break down his barrier of privacy. 'You should write fiction, *señorita*, you have a gift for it!'

'It's the truth!' His sarcasm stung like a lash, and she was far more affected by it than she liked to admit. Her hands were shaking and she needed every ounce of self-possession she could summon as she got up from the table. 'And if you'll excuse me, I don't want any more breakfast, I'd rather sit in my room until you're ready to start work.'

'And I'd rather you stayed where you are,' Manuel told her coolly. 'Or do you lack the courage of your convictions, Señorita Roderigo? Is it easier to go and hide in your room rather than face the truth?'

Standing, she was able to look down at the top of his head, the thick red-gold hair curling slightly at the back and giving him a curiously and quite unexpectedly vulnerable look that was oddly affecting. He was to all appearances giving his whole attention his breakfast, but

there was something about the angle of his head and the
set of his shoulders that suggested he was more aware of
her than his attitude implied.

'I've already faced the truth,' she told him, husky-
voiced and wary. 'You don't approve of what I do for a
living, and you resent the fact that I got the better of you
on a couple of occasions. What more is there?'

When he didn't reply she hesitated whether or not to
leave as she had planned to do and go back to her room,
but instead she walked across and stood in the curve of
the big window with her back to him. All she could see
out there was the deserted courtyard, bereft of gardens
and trees, and its fountain silent and lifeless, seeming to
reflect some of her own mood with its air of melancholy.
Having insisted that she stay Manuel got on with his meal
and completely ignored her, so that eventually she found
the silence unnerving and attempted to end it.

'I don't know what you want me to say,' she told him
without turning round, 'but whatever you think—
whatever you believe, I *was* just out for a drive that
day——'

'Ah, yes, in your cousin's car, you told me.'

'That's right, you know that.'

She half turned from the window and looked at him,
but he was still seemingly more interested in his meal
than in what she was saying, and he didn't look up. 'I
should have seen the light the moment I saw the car you
were driving,' he said, and sounded as if he was choosing
his words carefully. 'It did cross my mind when I crossed
the road to you that it was vaguely familiar, but it wasn't
important enough at the time to trouble me, and I was
under the impression that you'd been hurt——'

'I *had* been hurt,' Kristie insisted. 'You know that, you
saw the bruise on my forehead and suggested I should see
a doctor!'

'A small injury that you might have considered worthwhile inflicting on yourself if it helped you get your story!'
He dismissed her reasoning as he seemed to dismiss everything she tried to say to explain her position. 'It was only

when a lot of other details began to fall into place that I thought about the car again, and realised why I'd thought it looked familiar. You were in it when you came to the villa that first time, only your cousin was driving it then.'

'I—I didn't think about that,' Kristie confessed.

She didn't turn round again, but kept on looking out at the stark emptiness of the courtyard and the lifeless fountain, listening to the whisper of the wind through the archways, sounding as mournful as her own thoughts. Only when she heard Manuel get up from the table did she concentrate her whole mind on what he was doing instead. Hearing his firm, quiet tread as he came and stood immediately behind her so that the heat of his body warmed her back through the thin cotton dress she was wearing.

'There were quite a number of things you didn't think about,' he told her with menacing quietness, 'once you were convinced I didn't connect the reporter with the girl on the road. Small, insignificant things on their own, but significant enough to tell me how neatly I'd been fooled— once I got on to the one, unmistakable clue that I couldn't overlook! For instance, most people, and particularly an English woman, would assume a secretary to be female, yet you quite naturally referred to the temporary one I'd hired as "he". Suggesting that you knew something about him.'

'I know him.' Kristie turned round to face him because she was anxious to convince him that Marcos Francisco knew nothing about her plan. 'He's a friend of my cousin's and mine, but he knew nothing about my being interested in you. All he did was mention that when he came to the villa for an interview he saw someone who looked remarkably like Montevio.'

'Which was quite enough for you, of course!' Manuel guessed, then went on with the same relentless insistence as before. 'And you'd have given yourself away when you suggested I was writing my autobiography, if I hadn't already realised who you really were. Then there was Juan, your cousin, the same name you called the driver of the car you were in when you called at the villa the first time. Nothing very significant taken individually, but you see I'd already seen and recognised the one thing you couldn't disguise, or else were so accustomed to that you forgot about it.'

Dazed and unable to follow his meaning, Kristie stared at him. The stone window ledge pressed against the back of her thighs and prevented her from backing away from him any farther, and she cried out in genuine alarm when he thrust both hands into the neck of her dress and wrenched the two halves apart, exposing the first gentle swell of her breasts.

'*That's* what gave you away, Señorita Roderigo!'

Quite clearly on the pale skin of her left breast a faint pink scar showed; no more than an inch long and no thicker than a thread. It was the aftermath of a childhood accident, and he was right, she had grown so accustomed to the slight blemish that it did not even deter her from wearing low-cut dresses, like the one she had worn that day in the café. But never before had she felt so selfconscious about it as she did with his hard angry eyes fixed on it.

'You sat there with one hand at the neck of your dress,' Manuel went on, and the harshness of his voice suggested how bitterly he had been disillusioned that day, 'and I noticed you had a scar on your breast. I noted it because it seemed so wicked for anything so perfect to be even slightly blemished; and then I remembered where I'd seen it before!' His fingers still gripped the neck of her dress and she could feel the anger burning in him so fiercely it stunned her. 'I saw the same mark when your shirt was pulled open, when you came disguised as a boy, and once I had seen it the other pieces began to fall into place as you talked. I knew you'd never be able to resist offering to take the temporary's place and I let you walk right in—it was irresistible!'

He let go her dress with a gesture of disgust, and Kristie was too confused to know which emotion was uppermost as she refastened the two halves of the neck with trembling

hands. 'You have no right to say *I'm* devious,' she accused
in a shakily husky voice, and through the haze of tears
she saw the bitter resentment in his eyes and shivered.

She was sure he hated her with the fury of a proud
man who has allowed himself to be fooled. He had allowed
himself to be attracted for a while by a pretty face and he
despised himself for his moment of weakness almost as
much as he despised her. She felt out of her depth and
could see no way out at the moment, and it was quite
instinctive when she made her appeal.

'What—what are you going to do with me?' she asked,
and his sudden harsh bark of laughter made her jump.

'Work you, as I promised,' he told her. 'I have nothing
else in mind for you at the moment, Señorita Roderigo,
but——'

He shrugged and the look in his eyes sent a thrill of
coldness down the length of her spine. 'You wouldn't
dare!' she whispered, and knew before the words were out
of her mouth that she had made yet another mistake.

'You're either very bold or very naïve.' He was so close
that she could see every fine line that fanned from the
corners of his eyes, and the hard, set straightness of his
mouth. 'What do you imagine you can do to prevent me
doing anything I choose to do with you, Señorita
Roderigo? Over thirty kilometres from Seville and no one
in this practically deserted castle but you and me and
José, who incidentally is also conveniently deaf when he
chooses to be. What can you do, eh?'

There was nothing she could do, Kristie realised, and
yet it wasn't fear that stirred the pulse at her temple, nor
dismay either, but a curious kind of excitement. She knew
virtually nothing about him, and yet she wasn't afraid
of him as she perhaps ought to be; he had strength and
virility and he was angry enough to take revenge, but
still she wasn't afraid of what he might do to her.

'I can't do anything,' she admitted in a husky little
voice. 'But I don't believe you will either.'

She hadn't meant it to sound quite so much like a challenge, and she saw the dark gleam in his eyes as they

narrowed slightly. 'So,' he said softly; 'you think you know men, do you?'

He moved quickly and there was no time to evade him as he gripped her hard, drawing her into his arms and holding her to the bold vigorous length of him, pressing her so close she could feel every straining muscle in his body. Deafened by the thudding of her own heart, Kristie turned her head from side to side in automatic denial of her own response.

'I didn't say——' she began, but he cut her short, his voice roughly seductive.

'I know exactly what you said,' he declared, and his breath lifted the wisps of hair on her forehead.

As he spoke he pulled her closer still until the hard virility of his body taunted her with its nearness, and his hands sought the yielding softness of her breast. It was instinct alone that made her turn her face to the lure of his mouth, but she found not only passion there, but a fierceness that amounted almost to cruelty and made it not merely a kiss but a violent attack on her emotions.

At first she yielded, because it was what instinct made her do, but then she began to struggle against the steely strength of his arms, and the mouth that refused to let her go even when her head was spinning and her breathing became short and uneven. Pushing her hands against his chest, she sought to break the cruel dominance of his mouth, squirming wildly to escape.

It seemed like hours before he let her go and she was so lightheaded that for a few moments she stood breathing hard and with her hands pressed against his chest. With her eyes closed, she could still feel the bruising hardness of his kiss on her lips, and she shook her head when his hands moved slowly to hold her upper arms. It was a moment or two before she at last opened her eyes and found herself looking at a long length of brown throat where the usually steady pulse beat hard and fast.

She didn't know what she would have said to him when she raised her eyes and looked at him at last, but as he so often did, Manuel got in first. 'I feel we've wasted enough

time for one day,' he observed in a flat hard voice. 'I
suggest we start work if you've had all the breakfast you
want, Señorita Roderigo.'

He turned about and walked off across the room, leaving her still trembling like a leaf and standing in the curve
of the window staring after him. Then very deliberately
she turned and picked up a light copper vase and threw it
with staggering accuracy after him; as it struck the door-
frame right beside his head, he paused, but that was all.
To Kristie's chagrin he didn't even turn his head, but
went out and closed the door quietly behind him.

After three days of working flat out and without the customary breaks during morning and afternoon, Kristie was
becoming quite used to the more arduous routine, although she had never before felt so tired at the end of the
working day. But she was young and healthy, and she
told herself whenever she started to flag that hard work
had never killed anyone yet, and the last thing she
intended doing was complain to Manuel. Several times
she had noticed him look across at her when he thought
she was unaware of it, and she felt certain he was looking
for some sign of her weakening.

They said very little to one another, mostly, she guessed,
because they had little in common and because he did
not intend giving her a chance of getting to know him
any better and adding to the scant knowledge she already
had. During mealtimes they called a kind of truce, but
conversation was limited to what they had done that day,
or what Manuel proposed doing the next day, so that
Kristie, with her fondness for company, missed having
someone to talk to.

That was why, although he couldn't literally talk to
her, she sought the company of José in the kitchen. What
Manuel would have to say about it if he ever found out,
she didn't bother about unduly, but as José seemed not to
mind the first time, she took it she was free to go again.
Dinner was never very early, and there was plenty of time
between when they finished work for the day and dinner-

time to wash and change and still be able to visit the kitchen.

There was a certain reserve in José's manner, and Kristie had no doubt at all that he was absolutely loyal to Manuel, but it was plain from the warmth in his eyes when she walked in that he wasn't averse to having a pretty girl in his kitchen. On the first two occasions it had been much earlier when she came and she had persuaded José to give her something to tide her over until dinnertime, but this evening she was later and it was really too near the evening meal to eat anything beforehand.

Nevertheless when José handed her a bread roll, split and buttered and liberally spread with some kind of pâté, she hadn't the heart to refuse. *'Very special'* he wrote on the jotter he kept by him for writing down things he couldn't convey with his customary hand-signs, and she smiled.

In fact when she tasted it it seemed to have a rather gamey taste, but again she didn't like to criticise when he obviously meant to please her, so she nodded. 'It's very good, José, did you make it?'

He shook his head, using his hands, as he always did, to disclaim credit. *'From a friend'* he wrote, and she smiled as she bit once more into the roll.

So far they had never mentioned Manuel, mostly because Kristie had a feeling that José wouldn't tell her anything even if he knew. But now that she was beginning to know him better, and he seemingly liked her, she was very tempted to try, and see what the result was. Sitting on the edge of the kitchen table where he was working, she ate the roll slowly while she watched him prepare vegetables for tomorrow's *gazpacho*.

'José.' She brushed crumbs from the corner of her mouth, aware that his black eyes glanced at her curiously. 'How long have you known Señor Montevio? Oh, it's all right,' she added hastily when he showed surprise at her use of Manuel's proper name, 'I know who he is, I knew before I came here, so you won't be giving anything away.'

'*Does he know you know?*' José scribbled hastily, and she nodded.

'He knows. In fact, it's because he knows that I know that I'm here really.' Quite clearly he was puzzled, and Kristie couldn't really blame him, though it suggested that Manuel hadn't told him the real reason for her being there and she found that vaguely reassuring somehow. '*Have* you been with him very long, José?' she insisted, though he would obviously rather not have answered.

When he just went on chopping vegetables instead of answering her, Kristie began to think she had overstepped the mark and misjudged his reaction, but eventually he reached for the pencil and jotter and, as she popped the last of the roll into her mouth she leaned forward to see what he had written. '*Why do you ask?*' he wanted to know, and Kristie spread her hands in assumed nonchalance.

'Just because I find him interesting,' she said, and gave him what she hoped was a disarming wink. 'Our boss is a very attractive man, José, who wouldn't be interested, in my position?'

He wasn't entirely convinced, she thought, although he was nodding as if he understood and agreed with her opinion of Manuel Montevio, and he wrote once on the jotter. '*I've known him all his life. Thirty-four years.*' His sharp black eyes held hers for a moment, then he leaned forward and added a postscript. '*Too old for you.*'

He was taking her too literally for Kristie's comfort, and she coloured when she remembered that angrily passionate kiss of Manuel's; it had given rise to any number of wild and improbable fantasies since. 'Maybe you're right,' she allowed with a shivery little laugh, 'but he's still an interesting man. I remember when his picture used to be spread over all the sports pages and then suddenly—nothing, just as if he'd never existed. He disappeared completely and left half the world wondering where he'd disappeared to—and *why*.' Watching José's wrinkled dark face she tried to judge the mood of the man, but it had the same enigmatic blankness that Manuel's did sometimes. 'I'll bet you could tell me what suddenly made him

Join the Mills & Boon Reader Service and get much, much more, for a great deal less.

TAKE 4 FREE BOOKS EVERY MONTH

Romance
BITTER HOMECOMING
Jan MacLean

Mills & Boon Romance
HEARTBREAKER
Charlotte Lamb

Mills & Boon Romance
THE JUDAS KISS
Sally Wentworth

Mills & Boon Rom
BLUE DA AT SEA
Anne Wea

Turn the page for more exciting benefits

A sensational offer to readers of Mills & Boon, the world's largest publisher of romantic fiction.

Sorry to interrupt your enjoyment of this book for a moment, but we're sure you'd like to know about an exceptional offer from Mills & Boon.

Every month we publish ten brand new Romances – wonderful books that let you escape into a world of fascinating relationships and exciting locations.

And now, by becoming a member of the Mills & Boon Reader Service for just one year, you can receive *all ten* books hot off the presses each month–*but you only pay for six.*

That's right–four free books every month for 12 months. And as a member of the Reader Service you'll enjoy many other exclusive benefits:

✱ FREE monthly Newsletter packed with recipes, competitions and exclusive special offers.

✱ Brand new books delivered to your door–postage and packing FREE! No hidden extra charges.

✱ Friendly, personal attention from Reader Service Editor Susan Welland. Speak to her now on 01-684 2141 if you have any queries.

It's so easy! Send no money now–you don't even need a stamp. Just fill in and detach the reply card and send it off today.

14 DAY FREE TRIAL

Should you change your mind about subscribing, simply return your first ten books to us within 14 days and you will owe nothing.

Mills & Boon Reader Service, PO Box 236, Thornton Road, Croydon, Surrey CR9 3RU.

drop out of sight as he did, couldn't you, José? And why he's been in hiding ever since; not even using his own name any more. Why is it, José? Has he some deep, dark secret? A lot of people think it was something like that.'

José didn't even look up, he simply got on with what he was doing, as if his hearing as well as his speech was defective, and the effect of his silence was eventually so unnerving that she got up and walked over to the window. For several minutes she stood looking down at a steep hillside and miles of seemingly uninhabited countryside, then she turned again suddenly and looked at him.

'All right!' She gave a shivery little laugh. 'I'm an inquisitive woman—is it a crime?' José looked up at last, but his eyes were definitely wary when he studied her with disconcerting steadiness for a moment before using his hands in the same rapid way he did when he communicated with Manuel. 'Wait, please,' Kristie begged, and came hurrying across the huge kitchen again to stand beside him. 'Whatever it is you're trying to tell me, I can't understand you. Is it something about Manuel— Señor Montevio?'

He disclaimed that idea at once with a flurry of indignant gestures, then reached once more for the jotting pad. *Why do you want to know so much?* he wrote, and Kristie shook her head.

'I told you—because I find him an interesting man, and he's so reluctant to talk about himself.'

Once more he used the jotting pad, writing rapidly and at some length before thrusting it into her hands, then watching while she read. *He's suffered enough, don't make him go through all that again. Don't ask him about it, for the love of God.*

It was an impassioned plea and an affecting one, even scribbled in haste on a kitchen jotter, and Kristie found herself touched by it without having the least idea what it was about. Nor did she act like the journalist she always prided herself on being, and press for further information from José; she felt curiously anxious to impress him instead with her good intentions.

'I don't want to—to hurt him,' she insisted huskily. 'Whatever he thinks, that isn't what I want at all.'

It was a response that obviously puzzled him, for he was frowning curiously when he reached for the pad she still held in her hands. *'Who are you?'* his hasty scribble demanded, and Kristie looked down at her hands for a moment before she answered.

'I'm—I work for a newspaper.'

And that was enough for José, apparently, for he was nodding his head, and his eyes gleamed in very much the same way his employer's did sometimes. Then very deliberately he put down the pad on the kitchen table and walked away from her, a gesture so unmistakable that Kristie coloured furiously and felt suddenly quite alarmingly tearful.

She was still standing by the table and trying to think of some way to explain to José that in the present situation it was she who was the victim, not Manuel, when she heard the firm and unmistakable tread of Manuel's footsteps crossing the tiled floor in the hall. She glanced across to see if José had noticed too, and he glanced briefly in the direction of the door, but did not even look at her.

'I'd better go,' she said, but after another look at his uncommunicative back she shrugged resignedly and left; reluctantly, she had to admit.

Kristie always enjoyed a starter of grilled mushrooms and ham, so she didn't dream of attributing the curious feeling in her stomach to that; it was a kind of nausea, but she had never been allergic to mushrooms and had no reason to suppose there was anything different about these. She said nothing about it, but took a sip or two of wine and hoped it would go off after she'd eaten some of the sautéed vegetables that José had just brought in.

Conversation was always sparse, but she thought Manuel seemed unusually preoccupied, and once or twice she sensed him looking at her intently and was puzzled. It was several moments before she discovered what it was he had on his mind.

'José tells me you've been visiting him in the kitchen,' he said, and Kristie sighed inwardly at the inevitability of it.

'I suppose he told you about it somewhere in that jumble of hand signs you use,' she guessed, and not for the first time found herself resenting their having a means of communication that excluded her. 'You want to put a stop to it, I suppose?'

She thought it was inevitable that José would have told him about her interest in his past, and it was all the more surprising therefore when Manuel's reply proved her wrong. 'Not at all,' he told her. 'He simply said you wanted someone to talk to, and I can understand that. I suppose you find it a bit lonely up here, when you normally lead such a busy social life. I imagine it's necessary in your line of work.'

'It's not a mad social whirl by any means,' Kristie corrected him, 'but I do meet a fair amount of people and I miss the company. Also I like José, I can talk to him even though he has to write his answers on that pad he keeps in the kitchen.'

She still found it hard to believe that José hadn't given her away, and she was musing on that when she realised Manuel was still watching her between mouthfuls of dinner. She had noticed how he always allowed his gaze to drift down to the open neck of her dress, and it was the reason she had never again worn a neck low enough to show that betraying scar on her breast. It was the reason she now put a hand to her throat for a moment.

'I hope you're not thinking of José as a possible source of information,' he said. 'I would be very silly of you if you did, Señorita Roderigo.'

'It *would* be silly when I know he'd almost certainly tell you,' Kristie agreed, and his eyes narrowed slightly.

'I'm glad you realise it!'

She was tempted to let him know how wrong he was, but it wasn't as easy as she thought it would be to crow over him. Also it was becoming increasingly difficult to ignore the awful queasiness in her stomach, though she hoped she wouldn't have to let Manuel know; he might just think she was looking for sympathy.

'In fact I'm not too dimwitted to realise you'll have been trying to get around José,' Manuel said, and Kristie carefully avoided looking at him. 'He didn't say anything about it this time, I know, but he will if you persist, and you will, it's your nature, following the career you do.'

'You hate reporters, don't you?'

'I dislike having my own privacy invaded by the press,' Manuel agreed, 'although I know quite a lot of people in the public eye enjoy their attentions. Somehow I find it even less easy to like female reporters, and you're a particularly dangerous specimen, Señorita Roderigo, because you're a very pretty woman. Fortunately I'm confident that José can deal with you, and if he doesn't prove up to it, then I *can*. As a matter of interest, *are* there limits to what you'll do to get your story?' he added, and Kristie's reply had a rashness born of desperation.

'None at all,' she declared. 'Are there limits to what you'll do to prevent me getting it? For instance, if I did manage to get José to tell me your dark secret would you think up some fiendish revenge for both of us? After all, you are descended from the Borgia family, aren't you?'

It would have given her more satisfaction if he had at least looked up, but instead he went on eating, and Kristie's stomach rebelled at the sight of it. 'Who told you that?' he asked. 'Not José.'

'Isn't it true?'

He acknowledged it with a brief nod. 'It's true, although I still can't imagine where you picked up the information. Also if you know anything about the reputation of the Borgia, *señorita*, it should make you more careful how you behave while you're here. My notorious ancestors were not averse to poisoning their lovers to protect themselves, never mind their enemies.'

'And you count me an enemy!'

'Of course,' he agreed coolly.

It wasn't the kind of conversation that Kristie felt able to cope with in her present state. There was a bitter taste in her mouth and it was impossible to ignore the dreadful nausea in her stomach any longer. But hardest of all was trying to extricate the fact of her own present sickness from Manuel's talk of his Borgia ancestry, for the two seemed somehow to have become inextricably involved in her dazed mind.

When it eventually got to the point where she could no longer sit there and pretend there was nothing wrong, she put down her fork and got quickly to her feet, one hand pressed to her stomach and her face pale and beaded with perspiration. Manuel looked up curiously, then immediately left his seat, his expression anxious suddenly.

'Señorita Roderigo, what's wrong?'

Keeping a determined hold on her heaving stomach, Kristie couldn't resist a flash of macabre humour, though her voice almost wavered out of control. 'I ate dinner with a Borgia,' she whispered, then turned and ran quickly out of the room.

She was ill, horribly ill, but once it was over she had to admit she felt much better, even though she was rather weak and tearful. It was sheer determination that made her freshen herself up and while she washed and changed into her nightgown she longed for a comforting shoulder to lean on, and someone to assure her that the niggle of suspicion lurking in her mind couldn't possibly be true. Manuel Montevio was a harsh and revengeful man who was quite capable of making her work until she dropped, but how could she believe he was capable of anything like that?

She did not usually go to bed quite so early, but feeling as she was she decided it was the best place for her, although she didn't anticipate getting to sleep very easily with that uneasy suspicion still running around in her brain. Her only consolation was that if Manuel *had* attempted to follow in the footsteps of his notorious ancestors he had been much less efficient than they had been. And anyway, she told herself as her eyelids drooped, the whole idea was preposterous.

It could have been no more than ten minutes later that

she was snatched from a half-sleep by someone knocking on her bedroom door, and Kristie lay for a moment or two staring across the room. She licked her lips anxiously and her heart was hammering hard in her breast, for she had little doubt that it was Manuel, and as she sat up slowly he knocked again.

Picking up her robe from a chair, she got out of bed and padded barefoot across the room. Her pulse was racing and she was filled with such a tangle of emotions she couldn't think clearly. She was almost there when he knocked again, and called out to her. 'Señorita Roderigo, are you there?' The sound of his voice sent shivers along her spine, and she tried to bring her senses under control as she opened the door, running both hands through her hair as she looked at him.

The first thing he did was to run a disturbingly slow and intent gaze over her face, taking note of its paleness and of the wide, wary eyes that were quickly lowered, then he noticed that one hand held the light robe close under her chin, concealing the scar he always seemed to look for. It was a second or two before she realised he had a glass of brandy in one hand which he held out to her.

'This might help,' he suggested, but Kristie automatically shook her head as she took a step backwards into the room.

'Oh no, thank you!'

Manuel's eyes narrowed for a moment, then he shook his head. 'You must have been feeling terrible,' he said, 'but I didn't come before in case I embarrassed you. One doesn't really appreciate company, however well-intentioned, at a time like that, and especially a stranger. How do you feel now?'

'Oh—better, thank you.'

'The brandy will settle it completely—try it.' Once more he held out the glass to her, and again Kristie shook her head, backing away from him at the same time. Then she noticed his eyes narrow slightly between their thick golden lashes and briefly her pulse quickened again. 'Holy Mother of God!' he breathed softly. 'You actually believed all that Borgia nonsense!'

'No, of course I didn't!'

She denied it automatically, even though it was true, and as she turned and went back into her room she gave him a long look over her shoulder. It did not even occur to her that there was an invitation in the way she looked, and that she was virtually inviting him to follow her. With both hands around one of the tall wooden posts at the end of the bed she turned around in time to see Manuel tipping the contents of the brandy glass down his throat, and her fingers tightened on the polished wood when she realised how close he was.

'That should prove something, I think, don't you?' he asked, and she shook her head a little dazedly.

'It wasn't necessary.'

'Oh, but it was.' He glanced around the room, tilting the glass in one hand, then turned back and looked directly into her eyes. 'Shouldn't you order me to leave at this point?' he suggested quietly, and Kristie again shook her head.

'You've already told me that there's nothing I can do if you decide to—do whatever it is you have in mind,' she reminded him in a light and vaguely defiant voice, and Manuel eyed her for a moment steadily.

'This time the choice is yours.'

The softness of his voice was like silk and Kristie hastily suppressed a shiver. Whatever suspicions she had harboured earlier, her only thought now was that he was a far too disturbing visitor to have in her bedroom and if the choice really was hers she ought to ask him to go. He was much too attractive to have in such close proximity when she wasn't feeling as sure of herself as usual—and then there was that look in his eyes that she seemed to remember having seen before.

It was a deep, glowing look that seemed to see right into her soul, and made her feel alarmingly weak, and she recalled suddenly when she had seen it before. It had been when she glanced at him unexpectedly as she lay on the cot in the peasant woman's house after the accident, and again when he had admired her colouring when they sat together in the café before he realised who she was. A certain look that leaves a woman in no doubt that a man finds her desirable.

'Shall I go?' he asked softly, and Kristie found herself unable to send him away.

'I—I was wishing for company just before you came,' she confessed huskily, and he neither said nor did anything for a few moments, but held her eyes steadily.

Then he held out the empty brandy glass. 'I have the rest of the bottle in my room, if you'd like to change your mind,' he offered. 'That is if you trust me not to have doctored it, of course.'

Again Kristie shook her head. 'No, really, I'd rather nòt.'

'So——' He sighed deeply and with what she was sure was genuine regret. 'You still don't trust me.'

'Oh, but it isn't that at all,' she denied hastily. 'It's just that brandy doesn't agree with me; I go—funny.'

'I see!' His voice held a hint of amusement, but it slid like velvet down her spine, while his eyes strayed, inevitably it seemed, to the neck of her robe that was now open enough to show the scar he had made her so selfconscious about. 'Well, at least I can tell you what made you ill, and it had nothing to do with secret Borgia poisons. José gave you a roll with some pâté on, so he tells me.'

'That's right, he did, but——'

'The same one he gave me last week,' Manuel went on. 'I told him then that I thought it was a bit too far gone, so I can't imagine what made him give it to you. Because it was a very special one made by a friend of his, I suppose, and he didn't like throwing any of it away.'

A hand to her mouth, Kristie let out an audible sigh of relief. 'I never even thought about the pâté,' she confessed, and once more a gleam of slightly malicious amusement showed in Manuel's eyes for a moment.

'It made a much more dramatic story to suspect my Borgia ancestry of surfacing, naturally!'

'I—I'm sorry.'

She apologised without even stopping to think that by doing so she was admitting to having suspected him, but he seemed disinclined to make anything of it for the moment, and that too was a relief. She felt curiously limp as she clung to the support of the bedpost, and her face had a childlike quality without make-up and with dark smudges still under her eyes, and when she glanced up at him her mouth was tremblingly uncertain.

'I suppose you ate it because you didn't like to say no,' he guessed, and Kristie noticed that gentle look in his eyes again.

'I didn't want to hurt José's feelings,' she agreed, and Manuel shook his head.

There was something alarmingly sensual in the way he was looking at her suddenly so that she shivered and hastily lowered her eyes again. 'Ah,' he said softly, 'so you have a heart after all, eh?'

Standing there holding on to the bedpost, Kristie felt her whole body trembling and her legs were so weak they felt almost incapable of supporting her for much longer. It was such a temptation to sit down on the end of the bed instead, but she dared not; in this particular situation and with that look in his eyes, she dared not.

'You need some sleep, I'll leave you and let you get to bed.' He spoke very quietly and the suggestion made sense, but there was something in his voice that stirred a curious longing in her, and it was Kristie who shook her head slowly and almost without realising she was doing it.

'I'm not sleepy,' she denied in a breathless little whisper.

He was silent for a long moment, and while she stood there her heart was pounding so hard it seemed to make her whole body quiver with the force of it. Then he reached out and touched the corner of her mouth with a fingertip, stroking lightly over her lips until she half-closed her eyes and lifted her face to him.

'You should be,' he told her, and the deep softness of his voice was a caress in itself. 'You should send me away, you know that, don't you?' Kristie nodded without saying anything, but she made no move to ask him to go either, and after a moment or two his hands curved lightly about her cheeks while gleaming golden eyes looked down at her mouth with an intensity that stirred her blood. Then he placed his thumbs lightly on her lips and made a gentle stroking movement until she shivered uncontrollably. 'Kristie?'

It was a curious sensation, rather as if he was waiting, watching for a reaction, and just for a moment a tingle of warning slipped along her spine. She was a grown woman, she told herself, and if she wanted to bring the situation to an end she could do so there and then; only she didn't want to bring it to an end, whatever she ought to do.

Every nerve in her body was clamouring for him to take her in his arms and she couldn't think why he didn't when she offered no resistance. It was almost as if he expected her to turn him away, and she didn't understand why he should expect that. Then she looked up at him and the naked desire she saw in his eyes made it impossible for her to do anything but yield to her own wild longings as she lifted her arms and put them around his neck.

The touch of his body fired her senses and filled her with an indescribable need for him, and she shivered again when he drew her into his arms. Sliding his hands round behind her, he pressed them, flat-palmed, in the small of her back until his hard masculinity seemed to taunt her, and she tipped back her head.

His eyes were hidden, except for a narrowed slit of darkness between golden lashes, and their promise brought shudders of anticipation to her whole body, urging a response from her that she gave willingly. The light robe had fallen open and allowed her own soft flesh to touch the golden vee at the opening of his shirt, and long, firm fingers slid forward and upward, coaxing and persuasive, as she pressed closer.

She had a brief glimpse of glowing amber eyes and red-gold hair in the moment before his lips touched hers, and then nothing existed but the fury of desire that burned in the body and mouth that possessed her. Her robe parted and his mouth sought the softness of scented shoulders and a warm, pulsing throat before seeking out the pale scar on her breast and touching it lightly with his lips.

She welcomed his mouth again eagerly on hers, and when he eventually let her go, very slowly, she clung to his kiss for as long as she possibly could. Her parted lips were warm and tingling as he held her against the throbbing urgency of his heartbeat, and she turned her head instinctively to kiss the smooth golden skin where his shirt opened.

'Kristie?' She kept her head down and snuggled closer when he would have eased her away from him and very briefly his lips touched the nape of her neck. His voice, soft and slightly muffled by her hair, spoke close to her ear. 'It's as well you go home tomorrow,' he murmured, and Kristie looked up quickly, her eyes startled, shocked by the unexpectedness of it.

'But I'll be back again on Monday,' she said, and there was appeal in her voice as well as in her eyes. 'I'm standing in for three weeks, I must come back on Monday.'

Manuel put his big hands either side of her head, running his fingers through tangled fair hair, and there was a mingling of gentleness and desire in the way he looked at her. 'You must *not* come back on Monday,' he insisted. 'Don't you see, Kristie, where this could lead? I cannot have you here after this; I should not have had you here in the first place. When Esteban takes you home tomorrow, my dear, you won't come back again, it wouldn't be——'

His broad shoulders conveyed perfectly what kind of a situation he envisaged if she came back to the castle, but to Kristie it meant only that she would lose touch with him, and that was something she couldn't bear to contemplate at the moment. 'Oh, but you can't do that!' she protested. 'Manuel, you *can't* send me away, not now! Please, you can't!'

Manuel was holding her at arms' length and there was something in the shadowed mystery of his eyes that she didn't quite understand. 'I can and I will, for your sake,' he insisted, and it dawned on Kristie suddenly that there was a hint of disapproval in his manner.

'For my sake?' She laughed, and it was a light, husky sound filled with the strange new excitement that ran through her whole body and owed itself to those few moments in his arms. 'For my sake let me come back, Manuel! I don't care how hard I work, I'll work all the hours God made if you'll just let me stay with you—I *must* stay with you!'

'You must go home,' Manuel insisted. 'I can't be held responsible for what will happen if you come back here, Kristie, you must know that.'

'Please!' Her eyes had a soft, misty look that remembered nothing but the searing passion of his mouth on hers and the fierce strength of his arms; it was as if all else was forgotten or had never been. 'Don't you see,' she pleaded, 'I'm only just getting to know you? To really know you, and that's what I need to do more than anything. Let me go on working for you, eating with you, living with you, getting to—*know* you.'

'Know me!' Her head was still in the clouds and she sensed nothing wrong as she gazed at him with bright appealing eyes, only anxious that he shouldn't send her away from him. 'So you still haven't lost sight of your object!'

'Manuel?' She whispered his name; uncertain still but coming down to earth with every passing second. 'Isn't it natural that I want to know you better?'

'Of course!' His voice was harsh, unforgiving, like the glitter in his eyes as he looked down at her. 'How else would you get your story? I was surprised when you encouraged me to stay just now, but I was foolish enough to believe it was for a different reason than your damned story! I should have remembered that you've readily admitted to being prepared to go to any lengths to get it! I can only blame myself for allowing myself to be fooled yet again, Señorita Roderigo, but believe me this is the very last time! Goodnight!'

Kristie stared after him as he strode stiff-backed out of her room, and her eyes showed only stunned confusion for a moment. When realisation dawned it came swiftly and stunned her further so that she shook her head in swift denial. 'No!' It was a cry of pain as well as protest, but it was too late, for the damage had already been done by those pleading words that had meant something quite different, and Manuel was never going to believe her. He was never going to let those few tender, exciting moments happen again, and to Kristie, as she stood with tears filling her eyes, that mattered a lot more than getting her interview ever had.

CHAPTER SIX

It was fairly late when Kristie eventually woke the following morning, and she felt so heavy-eyed and unhappy that she very nearly decided to remain where she was. It wasn't easy to admit that since last night Manuel Montevio had become more important to her as a man than as the subject of an interview, but in her heart she knew it was true.

The actual length of time she had known him wasn't very much, but their acquaintance had been a stormy one from the beginning, and she felt herself more involved with him than she had ever been with a man before, even Juan. Juan was charming and they had a close, comfortable relationship, but he had never touched her emotions as Manuel did.

While she bathed and dressed she was going over the events of last evening. Had she ever seriously believed him responsible for her being so horribly sick? she wondered. Certainly she hadn't anticipated the effect of his kiss, or his insistence immediately afterwards that she must go home this morning and not come back. It was virtually all over unless she could devise some way of remaining there; not only her interview, but all contact with Manuel would be finished.

She was on her way to the head of the stairs, still hidden from sight to anyone down in the hall by a fretted balustrade and shadowed arches, when she heard voices and recognised one of them as Manuel's. 'See that the *señorita* takes *all* her belongings, Esteban.' The instruction reached her quite clearly, and a hasty glance down into the hall showed the chauffeur already at the foot of the stairs. 'Whatever she says to the contrary,' Manuel went on, obviously anticipating her resistance, 'the *señorita* will not be coming back, so see that nothing is left in her room!'

'Yes, *señor*.'

'José will be giving her breakfast in the kitchen this morning, and then we'll be leaving, and I want to be away by ten o'clock. Please tell her that too.'

'Of course, *señor*.'

He started on his way upstairs, but apparently Manuel still hadn't finished what he had to say and he called after him. 'If there is any difficulty,' he told the man grimly, 'come and tell me—I'll deal with it!'

Without doubt he intended getting rid of her once and for all, and clearly he was feeling no more kindly towards her this morning. It was in the blindness of desperation that Kristie made her next move, and her heart was pounding like a wild thing as she made quick, panicky plans to frustrate him.

There was nothing she could do to prevent the chauffeur taking all her belongings out of her room, but Manuel was mainly concerned with getting her personally away from the castle, and there might just be something she could do about that. Without stopping to consider the logic of what she was proposing to do, she turned quickly and slipped back along the corridor, only glancing at her bedroom door as she went hurrying on at a pace just short of a run. If she couldn't be found, she reasoned, she couldn't be sent home, and the longer she could remain unseen, the better her chances.

Whether or not José remained there or had a home of his own that he went to at weekends, she had no idea, but the thought of being stranded there alone did not deter her at the moment; she was only concerned with not being sent home for good. Right at the end of the main corridor another turned at right angles to it, and Kristie unhesitatingly turned into it and kept going.

It was new territory, somewhere she had never ventured before, and in the first few seconds, as she was enveloped in sudden darkness and chill, she slowed her pace. There were no windows and it grew even darker as she went on, also it smelled of damp and the mustiness of age, and was enough to discourage anyone.

But then somewhere behind her, and seeming a long way off, she recognised the sound of someone knocking on a door, and Esteban's voice seeking a response to his knocking. The almost empty castle echoed to every sound, carrying it around the chill corridor and adding to the sense of isolation as she went deeper into the windowless gloom, but she couldn't turn back now.

At the end of the corridor she found her way blocked by a door, and it was a moment or two before she could summon enough nerve to open it, for heaven knew what she would find on the other side. Eventually, with little alternative, she cautiously turned the handle and mentally cringed from the anticipated creak of ancient hinges. But it didn't happen, instead the heavy door swung silently inwards, and she was half blinded for a moment by a blaze of sunlight that came in through tall, glassless windows.

Obviously, from its shape and height, the room was contained in one of the turrets that gave the castle its impressive, all-conquering look, and she stood for a moment gazing around her. It was completely un-furnished and there would be nowhere to hide if they came looking for her, for a glance out of one of the windows showed only a narrow stone balcony surrounded by a low parapet—all that stood between her and the plunging depth of the chasm that had so impressed her when she drove there first. It wasn't the ideal hid-ing-place, but it would have to do; if Manuel was so determined to be rid of her, then he would have to come looking for her, for she would do nothing to co-operate.

Two hours later she wasn't quite so sure of her de-termination as she sat gazing out at the awe-inspiring scenery, and she could guess how angry Manuel would be getting by then. She got quickly to her feet when something she heard suggested that the search was not only still going on, but was getting too close for comfort suddenly. Watching the door and wondering where on earth she could go if it suddenly opened, she stood with her hands pressed over her mouth and her back to the window.

'Señorita Roderigo?' Manuel was obviously coming along that unlit corridor and, unless she misread the signs, he was every bit as furious as she had anticipated, so that she turned her head, seeking a way of escape. '*Señorita!*'

There was nowhere else but the narrow strip of balcony and Kristie wondered if she wasn't quite mad, going to such pains to stay where she wasn't wanted. He was getting closer and her heart thudded hard as she swung first one leg and then the other over the low sill, clinging to the steep outer wall that went soaring on upward over her head and not daring to look beyond the parapet.

There was very little space as she crouched there listening for Manuel and when he opened the door and his footsteps echoed on the stone floor, she held her breath. She heard him swear under his breath, probably because he had drawn another blank, then sensed him pause and frowned curiously when she recognised a faint sniff.

'*Señorita?*' He spoke softly and the lure of his voice tempted her for a moment, making her bite on her lip to resist answering him. 'Kristie!'

The sudden alarm in his voice startled her and she clung tightly to the rough stone wall, listening to him come striding quickly across the empty room. She ducked back as far as she could only just in time when he swung his long legs over the sill and leaned over the low parapet, murmuring something under his breath that sounded very much like a prayer.

Scarcely believing she was still undetected, she watched his face as he looked down into the plummeting depths of the chasm, and the expression she saw there stunned her for a moment. Only when he drew back and closed his eyes for a second in obvious relief did she realise what was in his mind, and she almost spoke up then, deterred at the last moment by his murmured thanks to a merciful deity.

Crouched as she was in the far corner of the balcony she seemingly remained unseen, although she couldn't imagine how, and she thankfully straightened her cramped limbs when she heard the door slam to after Manuel. Then, trembling like a leaf, she climbed back into the room and sat for a moment with her face in her hands. What happened next she had no idea, but she wished she need not have seen the look of anguish on his face as Manuel leaned over the parapet. She wouldn't knowingly have put anyone through that, and particularly not Manuel.

It was because she had checked her wristwatch so frequently that Kristie knew exactly how slowly the time had passed, just as she knew she could not stay where she was for very much longer. Whether or not the others had left in the car as scheduled, she constantly reassured herself that Manuel wouldn't go and leave her there alone. Whatever his faults he wasn't a callous man, but if he *was* still there he wasn't likely to be feeling very kindly disposed towards her.

Eventually it was hunger that moved her, and she rubbed a hand over her complaining stomach as she got to her feet. It had been her own fault that she missed breakfast, but it was getting on for lunchtime now and being so ill last night meant that her stomach was literally empty, and it was beginning to tell.

It was so quiet as she made her way back along the narrow dark corridor that she could almost believe there was no other living soul left in the castle but herself, and she shivered. She felt curiously lightheaded and her senses were consequently at a finer pitch than normal so that the whispering voice of the wind seemed more alarming than usual, and she increased her pace as she hurried along the main corridor.

Resisting the temptation to look into her own room, she hurried on downstairs, listening all the time for a sound of someone but hearing nothing, and as she approached the kitchen she called out, 'José!'

No one answered, and when she flung the door wide she found the kitchen deserted, but the table spread with the ingredients for making a *cocido*, and that alone was enough to boost her flagging spirits. Turning quickly, she tried the room they used as an office, but that too was deserted, and only one thing encouraged her. The cigarettes that Manuel smoked had a strong distinctive aroma and it lingered in the room; not a stale smell, but quite fresh, and enough to send her hurrying across to the *salón* she had occasionally shared with Manuel after work in the evening.

At first glance it too was unoccupied and her heart thudded hard in a sudden onset of panic. 'Oh no, he wouldn't!' she mourned, and all the anguish she felt at being abandoned was in her voice.

Even the gnawing ache in her stomach was briefly forgotten, although it was the weakness brought on by hunger that made her suddenly tearful as she walked on into the *salón*. She stopped dead in her tracks and brushed a hand across her eyes when she saw Manuel standing with his back to her, and the smoke from a cigarette wisping up round that distinctive red-gold head.

Because her legs were suddenly too weak to support her, she clutched the edge of the door, and her head was swimming as she gazed across at him. All that mattered at the moment was that he hadn't abandoned her after all, and while she still stood looking at him with undisguised relief, he turned slowly and levelled that disturbing gaze at her.

'So,' he said quietly, 'you eventually decided you'd had enough of your turret and came out of hiding.'

Trying to gather her wits together, Kristie shook her head. 'How—how did you know where I was?'

He drew on his cigarette before he enlightened her, and she was reminded of that faint sniff she had heard as she crouched outside the window. 'Your perfume,' Manuel informed her in a flat, hard voice. 'I have good reason to remember it!'

She accepted the fact that he could be coldly sarcastic

about last night, but it hurt none the less. 'I didn't—I didn't intend to give you the idea that I'd—I'd gone over the parapet,' she whispered, and knew as soon as she had said it that he was going to resent her having witnessed that moment of anguish. 'I'm sorry.'

His eyes were sharply glittering, yet at the same time oddly evasive, and he drew again on the cigarette, expelling a long plume of smoke from between pursed lips. 'You're just fool enough to have tried to scale the turret wall in an attempt to stay here at all costs,' he remarked in the same flat voice. 'I find it hard to believe that even you will go to these lengths to stay on the job! But you just won't give up that damned interview, will you? Not if you disrupt everyone's arrangements and risk breaking your neck to get it!'

Kristie wanted to tell him that he had it all wrong; that she wasn't nearly so concerned with getting her interview as with trying to make him understand her reason for pleading with him to let her stay last night. Whether she could ever convince him seemed doubtful when she took note of his set mouth and the gleaming harshness of his eyes, and she didn't feel able to cope with anything much at the moment.

Her head felt alarmingly light and floaty as she passed a moistening tongue over her lips, and her voice seemed to come from a long way off. 'It—it wasn't because of the interview,' she began.

'And I am supposed to believe that? Just for once do me the favour of not treating me like a fool,' Manuel told her, and came across the room as he spoke. Standing immediately in front of her he brought that stunningly affecting aura of masculinity to trouble her already fuddled senses and she tried hard to gather her wandering wits. 'You've put me and my staff to a hell of a lot of trouble, Señorita Roderigo,' he went on, 'and I don't take kindly to having my plans disrupted. Thanks to you I'm here instead of at home in Seville!'

'I'm sorry,' she murmured faintly. 'Isn't Esteban coming back for you?'

'You think I put everyone about for my own convenience as well?' Manuel demanded, and the violence with which he ground out the stub of his cigarette made her shiver. 'It obviously didn't concern you that there were other people to consider,' he went on. 'My mother was expecting me home, and José has a daughter he spends the occasional weekend with. Esteban, whom you so blithely suggest should come back for me, has a wife and family, and your own family would no doubt have wondered what had happened to you if I hadn't asked Esteban to take them a message.'

Appalled at her own thoughtlessness, Kristie shook her head. 'I—I didn't think,' she said, and Manuel gave a harsh snort of derision.

'I doubt if you very often *do* think!' he declared harshly. 'When you have your mind set on chasing a story I imagine nothing else matters to you. However, if you're having a belated twinge of conscience about your aunt, I've written her a note and explained that as we're rather busy we shall be staying here over the weekend, and that she has nothing to worry about. It would, of course, have sounded better coming from you, but we can only hope she will accept my explanation and not worry too much!'

It was the final straw, realising that she hadn't given Aunt Maria a thought, and Kristie caught her lip between her teeth for a moment as she coped with another wave of dizziness. 'Thank you,' she murmured.

He glared at her in silence for a moment, then made a sharp, impatient 'tcch!' and jerked one hand in a gesture of dismissal. 'I still can't understand anyone risking being locked in an empty castle for the weekend. Suppose you *had* been alone, what good would it have done you?'

'Oh, but I knew you wouldn't go and leave me here!'

Manuel narrowed his eyes and glared at her. 'Oh, you did?'

'I—I hoped you wouldn't.'

Her voice was growing more unsteady, and she felt alarmingly dizzy as the gnawing pangs of hunger forced themselves on her notice again. Worst of all she felt like crying, and when she blinked her eyes the tears actually fuzzed her vision for a moment, and trembled on her lashes as she looked up at him in sudden alarm. For she had the awful conviction that any moment now she was going to fall at his feet in a faint, and for no better reason than that she had gone hungry far too long. 'Manuel,' she said faintly, 'I think I'm——'

'You're an excellent judge of men, Señorita Roderigo,' he interrupted, referring to her conviction that he wouldn't go and leave her there alone. 'I couldn't simply go back to Seville, knowing you were still here, but that is as far as my compassion goes! Don't imagine this little scheme is going to do anything for you at all; last night was enough to convince me that you really will stop at nothing, and this morning my eyes are wide open! Your tears don't impress me, and nor do those big, appealing eyes! In the kitchen you'll find everything you need to make a meal, José left it ready, and you'd better be able to cook, my girl, because if you can't neither of us is going to eat this weekend, and I'm even less amiable when I'm hungry!'

'I—I can cook.' It wouldn't be long now, she knew, before she had no option but to succumb to the buzzing, head-spinning faintness that made it hard for her to go on standing there, and she put a hand to the nauseous void in her stomach as she felt herself sway. 'I—I think I'm going to——'

'You don't fool me,' Manuel declared sharply. 'You know where the kitchen is, *señorita*, I suggest you make a start!'

'Manuel——'

She got no further, for her head was filled with a loud rushing noise suddenly and she felt as if it was leaving her body, so that when she swayed instinctively towards Manuel, there was nothing she could do about it. Swiftly he reached out and caught her in his arms, holding her for a moment while he looked down into her face, still suspicious, until the vague look in her eyes convinced him she wasn't faking. Then he lifted her into his arms and carried her to one of the armchairs, setting her down gently, then bending over her.

'Kristie?' A big hand was laid lightly against her cheek. 'Are you ill?'

It wasn't easy to concentrate, for the face above her kept swimming in and out of vision, but Kristie did as well as she could, and even attempted a reasssuring smile. 'Not—not ill,' she murmured, 'just—just hungry.'

'Holy Mother!'

He swore softly, and just for a moment Kristie feared he might suspect it was a trick after all, which was why she tried to explain as best she could for a head that kept floating away from her body and made it very hard to concentrate. 'I didn't have breakfast, and—and—last night——'

'You little *fool*!' Manuel interrupted fiercely. 'How can you be so completely idiotic? You take more risks for that damned job—tcch! You aren't fit to be allowed out alone!' Kristie said nothing; she was incapable at the moment of thinking clearly enough to put two words together, but she couldn't help taking a strange comfort from his anger, and she did her best to focus her gaze on him when he straightened up suddenly. 'Stay where you are,' he told her firmly. 'I can manage to make a sandwich to keep you going until we have a proper meal, but——' He leaned down and placed a hand on each arm of her chair, 'this does not excuse you preparing and cooking the rest of the meals, is that understood?'

Kristie nodded, her head swimming. 'Yes,' she breathed.

'Then stay there while I make a sandwich, and don't dare move!'

Leaning back in her chair, Kristie watched him go stalking out of the room, and she felt strangely contented despite her aching, spinning head and the sickening void of hunger in her stomach. She had achieved her object in so far as she was still with Manuel, and who knew what opportunities the weekend might present?

There wasn't time to make *cocido* for lunchtime, so Kristie did her best with what was available and the time she had. A sandwich and a huge cup of black coffee had worked wonders, and Manuel sat and watched her while she took the edge off her hunger, unable to conceal a faint smile when she heaved a sigh of satisfaction as she finished.

But he had been adamant about her taking over kitchen duties, and as soon as he was satisfied that she was fit again, he ordered her into the kitchen. It wasn't as lavish a meal as José usually presented for lunch, but it was good enough at a moment's notice, and Manuel made no complaint.

Chilled fruit juice made an easy first course, and although cooking wasn't really her strong point, she produced some very passable ham and cheese omelettes to eat with a salad, followed by grilled lamb chops with mushrooms, peas and rice, and icecream to finish. The coffee she made thick and black the way Manuel liked it, and altogether she felt she had done fairly well at her first attempt.

Neither of them had said very much during lunch, and as she scooped up the last of her icecream she gave Manuel a sidelong glance. 'Have you had enough to eat?' she asked, and he nodded.

'Yes, thank you.' Having already finished his meal he helped himself to coffee, then sat with his elbows resting on the table and his fingers steepled, supporting his chin. He was studying her intently and, because she found it too disturbing, Kristie went on scraping away at her empty dish rather than look up again. 'I'm glad to find you have at least one feminine asset,' he told her. 'That omelette was excellent; even José couldn't have faulted you there, and the chops were grilled to perfection.'

'Thank you!'

Kristie was appalled to realise that she had coloured

like a schoolgirl and, because there was nothing she could do to hide it, she went on scraping her empty bowl until a large hand was pressed over hers. She looked up automatically and caught a faint glimmer of amusement in his eyes that was as unexpected as the touch of his hand.

'Does it make you blush to be complimented on your cooking?' Manuel asked, and she recalled how once before he had commented on her blushing. On that occasion too he had smiled faintly, just as he did now, only the smile then had been more gentle and less mocking.

'You seem to find it cause for remark because I sometimes feel embarrassed enough to blush,' she told him. 'You spoke about it once before.'

'I did?' He mused for a moment, then nodded. 'Ah yes, I remember, it was when I suggested that you had no need to worry about eating pastries, wasn't it? But that was before I knew who and what you were, and the fact that you blush is even more remarkable now.'

'Because I'm a hard-boiled reporter, you mean?'

His eyes were heavy-lidded and very hard to read, and he heaved his broad shoulders in a shrug. 'I hadn't seen you as a woman who would know how to cook either,' he observed.

Determined to treat it lightly and not be goaded into losing her temper, Kristie eyed him with her head on one side and a hint of a smile on her mouth. 'Hence the blush,' she told him. 'I'm not used to being complimented on my cooking!'

'You don't consider it necessary for a woman to know how to cook?'

The softness of his voice was a deceit, Kristie felt sure, for he could not already have forgotten his anger at being deprived of his weekend at home, and she eyed him warily before she replied. 'It depends,' she said, 'on her circumstances. I mean, where's the point of learning if you're never likely to have to cook? Why bother, for instance, if you've an even chance of winding up married to a millionare?'

Manuel had picked up his glass and he sat for a moment

gazing down at the wine in the bottom of it, swirling round and round like liquid gold. Then he took a long drink, and the softness of his voice when he answered her played havoc with her senses, however firmly she told herself only a fool would allow herself to be so affected.

'So you mean to marry a millionaire, do you?' he asked, and to her dismay Kristie again felt herself blushing.

'I didn't say that,' she denied. 'I'm not interested in marrying anyone at the moment, and it's highly unlikely it will be a millionaire when I do!'

'But you live in hope?' Manuel suggested softly, and she looked up quickly. 'Have you found him yet?' he wanted to know. 'Or don't you move in such exalted circles?'

'You're the first one I've met!'

The retort had been irresistible, but she knew it had been a mistake when she noticed the way his eyes narrowed slightly as he put down his wine glass with almost studied care. 'I'm sorry to disappoint you, Señorita Roderigo,' he said quietly, 'but I'm not quite in the millionaire class.'

Because he seemed to be challenging her, Kristie couldn't resist reacting as she did, and she angled her chin as she looked at him. 'I find that hard to believe, with your life-style,' she told him. 'A villa in Seville, a castle in the mountains and always someone at your beck and call—you seem to do pretty well, *señor!*'

Manuel regarded her steadily for a moment and a small tingling shiver slipped along her spine. 'But not nearly well enough to suit you, my dear *señorita*,' he said. 'Don't give up cooking yet, for you've got the wrong man. Tempting as you were last night I'm afraid you were wasting your time, whether it was done to get your precious information for your feature article or to capture a millionaire husband. Like you, I'm not interested in marrying at the moment.'

Kristie stared at him in blank disbelief, for this latest accusation was completely unexpected and uncalled for. Then once more her cheeks flooded with hot, bright colour brought on in this instance by rising anger, and she glared at him furiously as she got to her feet. The blood was pounding in her head and she was trembling like a leaf.

'You—conceited, arrogant, bigoted——'

'Take care!' Manuel warned softly, but Kristie was past being warned and she went on heedlessly.

'For your information, Señor Montevio, I wasn't concerned with either getting material for my article *or* in trapping you into marriage last night! I was feeling very sorry for myself and not fully recovered from that wretched sickness or I'd never have let you past the door! You have no right to talk about me as if I was some—some woman you'd picked up in the street, and I strongly object to it!'

'I said no such thing,' Manuel insisted, and the fact that he did not even raise his voice made her even more angry.

'You implied it! In fact it was you who started it all when you just—walked in!'

'That may be true,' Manuel conceded coolly, 'but I fully expected to be asked to leave again, not given a look that would have undermined the resolve of any man worthy of the name. I didn't realise at the time, of course, that it was all part and parcel of your attempt to—get at?—me.'

'It *wasn't*!' She felt as desperate to convince him now as she had ever been, but he was obviously no more likely to be convinced. 'Oh, why won't you believe that I'm not on the job every hour of the day and night?'

'Because you've never given me cause to believe you're not.'

Kristie swallowed hard, trying to bring a logical mind to bear but finding it too difficult. 'You suspect everything I say and do,' she said and her voice had a husky, slightly wavery sound as she clasped her hands tightly together. 'I don't know what reason you had for dropping out of sight the way you did, but it must have been pretty—traumatic to make you as suspicious as you are.'

When he got to his feet the tension had never been

greater between them, but something in his eyes touched
her without her being sure why, so that she felt a sudden
need to back off, and she shook her head slowly. 'I dislike
being hounded,' Manuel said, 'and I object to having my
privacy invaded, does that make me some kind of a freak?'
This time she shook her head to deny the suggestion that
he was any kind of a freak, but he took no more notice of
that than he did of her verbal denials. 'I honestly cannot
understand a young woman with looks and charm who
feels such a compulsion to spread my private affairs in
front of the public that she will risk being locked up in a
deserted castle all weekend rather than give up.'

'But that had nothing to do with my job!'

His lower lip pursed scornfully and he looked down at
her with heavy-lidded eyes. 'Oh, please, my dear *señorita*!'

Kristie almost choked on her words, for she was close to
tears, and crying was the last thing she wanted to do in
the present situation. He would never believe they were
caused by his bad opinion of her. 'You'll never believe
me,' she said despairingly. 'You simply can't forgive me
for being what I am. Most of all you can't forget you
were once fooled into thinking I was another girl
altogether, and you blame me for that too!' Her voice
rose with the realisation that she was getting nowhere,
and she once more swallowed hard on the encroaching
tears. 'Well, stick to your suspicions and your—your sec-
rets! I promise you that for the rest of the weekend I
won't come near you, nor will I ever again!'

The brief glimpse she had of his face showed his eyes
narrowed and speculating, and she clenched her hands
tightly at the thought of him still not accepting her word.
'You're giving up?' Manuel asked, and she felt too choked
for a moment to answer him.

'I haven't any choice,' she said eventually in a small,
shaky voice, and just for a moment looked up at him
again. 'And don't worry, I'll cook the meals, as I said I
would, but I'll eat mine in the kitchen so that you won't
have to suffer my company.'

'In the name of heaven, don't be such a little fool!'

So now he was angry again, but for quite a different reason, and Kristie brushed a hand across her eyes before she looked at him. Her heart felt like a lead weight and she wanted more than anything to forget those few minutes in her room last night, but found it impossible. That kiss had made too much impression on her, and whatever he said or did to her she knew she would never forget. How could he have so misunderstood her?—then or now.

'I *was* a fool,' she allowed huskily, 'but I won't be again—ever.' She walked acrosss the room on legs that felt almost too weak to carry her, and when she turned in the doorway it was only for a second, and she studiously avoided looking at him directly. 'I'll have the meal ready at the usual time,' she promised. 'In the meantime I'll stay out of your way.'

He didn't reply, but as she closed the door behind her Kristie wondered just how deeply he had resented hearing a few home truths about himself, for it couldn't happen very often. Only when she had gained the privacy of her own room did she give way to the despair she felt, and burst into bitter tears; crying as she had never cried in her life before. And all over a man she was convinced despised her more than ever.

Her eyes were still a little puffy, but Kristie was resigned rather than content as she prepared the evening meal, and when the *cocido* turned out as well as the lunchtime omelettes had done, she wondered vaguely if she might not have a gift for cooking. Manuel would naturally consider it a much more suitable occupation for a young woman than journalism, but then Manuel was opinionated to the point of bigotry.

She was dishing up the fragrant mixture of lamb, sausage and various vegetables, ladling off the liquid to use as a first course soup, and she didn't bother to look around when the kitchen door opened. It could only be Manuel and she didn't feel like facing him again just yet, so she gave no sign at all that she knew he was there but gave all her attention to what she was doing. It was inevitable, she supposed ruefully, that her hand would shake when he came up behind her and some of the soup splash over the side of the bowl.

Apparently he noticed the place she had set for herself on the kitchen table, for she heard his tongue cluck impatiently and then followed the rattle of cutlery as he displaced the pieces with a sweep of his hand. 'You can't intend to carry on with that nonsense of eating in the kitchen,' he declared. 'You'll eat with me as usual.'

'I think it's better if I eat in here.'

She didn't stress it too much, because if it came to an argument about it she knew only too well that she would yield, and inevitably he disagreed. 'It's nonsense and you know it!'

Kristie went on ladling out soup and she still didn't look at him; her cheeks were flushed from the heat of the stove, but it wasn't the only reason her colour was so high. And it certainly didn't account for the almost choking beat of her heart as she set the bowl to one side for a moment while she put the *cocido* on the hot-plate to keep warm.

'Are you ready for your soup now?'

'If you are.' She couldn't stand and defy him with their lunch ready to serve, so she nodded, and he took the bowl of soup from her. 'I'll carry it in,' he said in a voice that brooked no argument. 'You go ahead and set a place for yourself in the dining-room. And please don't argue,' he added as he herded her across the kitchen in front of him, 'I'm hungry and I want my dinner!'

In fact she didn't want to argue with him, Kristie realised, though she didn't intend to yield too obviously either. 'I thought I'd made it clear that I intended to stay out of your way,' she told him, but Manuel huffed derisively.

'You made it clear that you were making a gesture,' he informed her. 'There's no need for it, and you'll eat with me as you have before. Now please set another place and let's get on with dinner before the soup cools too much.'

He was bound to have the last word, of course, and Kristie led the way into the dining *salón*, taking extra cutlery from the sideboard and setting her place right next to Manuel's, as José always did. She wished she could have relaxed while they ate their meal, but somehow she couldn't, and she was too conscious of him there beside her, knowing there were only the two of them in that vast empty castle.

The meal was even better than she anticipated, and it seemed inevitable when she coloured up on being told how good it was. 'And please don't tell me I'm blushing,' she told him in nervous haste before he could remark on it. 'You must realise by now that even reporters blush on occasion.'

'I wasn't going to say anything as provocative as that,' Manuel assured her, and the gravity of the words was in such direct contrast to the warmth of humour in his eyes that she could do nothing about the faintly reproachful half-smile she gave him.

'I'm very glad to hear it!'

'In fact,' he went on in the same quiet tone, 'I was about to suggest that we call a truce for the remainder of the weekend, otherwise it's going to be very uncomfortable for both of us.'

'I couldn't agree more!'

He responded with a slight smile that again warmed his eyes and sent a light, tingling sensation fluttering along her spine. There was so much about him that attracted her and the more she was with him, the more evident it became. Aside from her original need to learn all she could about him so that she could write a feature article, she now frankly admitted that as a man he intrigued her more and more. She still wanted to know all there was to know about him, but it was to satisfy her need as a woman, not as a journalist.

The meal finished, Manuel leaned forward on his elbows as he always did, but there was something in his manner that made her vaguely uneasy for a moment. 'Will your aunt be satisfied with my explanation, do you think?'

he asked, and Kristie looked at him for a moment before she replied.

'Almost certainly she will,' she said, while still trying to decide why he had suddenly decided to raise that subject. 'Aunt Maria is a nice, uncomplicated lady and it wouldn't occur to her that there was any other reason for me to stay on than that I had extra work to do. The fact that you wrote to her instead of me she'll probably see as a courtesy on your part, because you wanted me to work over the weekend.'

Manuel was holding his coffee cup between his hands and for the moment his lashes hid what was in his eyes. 'And your cousin—Juan?' he asked.

Kristie wished her hands weren't trembling so much, but she found it much harder to answer for Juan than for Aunt Maria. There was a difference in Juan lately that she had tried not to notice, but in her heart she knew why he looked at her the way he did sometimes. What puzzled her was why Manuel was interested.

'Oh, Juan takes things as they come for the most part,' she said, and sought to add conviction with a light shrug. 'He's very easy-going, like me.'

'He's very good-looking, judging by the little I've seen of him,' Manuel observed. 'You must make a handsome pair.'

She hated to think where he was leading her, so she trod cautiously; she didn't want any misunderstandings about her relationship with Juan. 'I don't think you'd describe us as a pair,' she told him. 'I mean, we don't live in each other's pockets, but we do go around together, usually with other friends.'

Those intriguing golden lashes still hid his eyes from her, and Kristie took advantage of it to study him for a moment. She felt sure there was something more than mere polite interest behind his conversation, yet she couldn't quite see what it was. 'Then there's no—romance in the air?' he asked, and Kristie instinctively shook her head.

'There's definitely no romance,' she insisted, but it

would have been much easier to deny it if she did not keep recalling the occasional deep-eyed looks that Juan had been giving her lately. 'We're cousins; second cousins actually, and we're good friends. Partly because we're much of an age, I suppose, and because we share a lot of the same tastes, although there are times when Juan doesn't approve of what I do any more than you do. But there's definitely no romance, take my word for it!'

'I have to take your word for it,' Manuel told her, and he raised his eyes at last. They were glowingly golden and much too affecting at such close quarters, so that her heart began the too familiar hard, rapid beat. 'I can't help wondering, though,' he went on, 'just how good a judge you are.'

'Of my own feelings?' Kristie asked, and he shook his head.

'Of your cousin's.'

It was becoming too personal, too difficult to go on being casual and matter-of-fact, and her hands moved restlessly while she spoke. Straightening the spoon in her saucer and the position of the cruet pieces on the table, 'I know Juan,' she vowed in a voice that sounded far less certain than the words she used. 'He might look at me as if I'm the only girl in the world sometimes, but that's something that the average Spanish male does as a matter of course, and is not to be taken seriously.'

'Never?' Manuel enquired softly, and she found herself blushing again.

'Well, of course it depends on the circumstances,' she allowed, but went no further to enlighten him; instead she looked at her watch and got to her feet at the same time. 'And being in sole charge of the kitchen means that I can't sit here waiting for somone else to come and clear away the dishes and wash them up,' she said. 'I'd better get on with it or it will be time for bed before I get started.'

Gathering up the empty dishes and cups, she stacked them all on to a tray and tried to pretend she was unaware of the fact that Manuel was watching her the whole time with that steady, heavy-lidded look that was so disconcerting. She was about to pick up the laden tray when he got to his feet and took it from her, laying his long brown fingers over hers for a moment and making her pulse jump violently.

He walked ahead of her into the kitchen and set the tray down on the draining-board, then turned and faced her, that same disturbing look in his eyes so that she hastily avoided them. 'Has it occurred to you that there will be no one else here tonight?' he asked, and a little warning shiver slipped along her back as she nodded. 'It doesn't—disturb you?'

What was he trying to make her say? Kristie wondered. It was such an obvious challenge that she looked up at last, and met his eyes as steadily as she was able to, though her heart was hammering. 'It was my own fault that I didn't go home,' she reminded him, 'I can't blame anyone else. And I'm sure you'll have told Aunt Maria that she has nothing to worry about.'

'But your aunt doesn't know me,' he said softly.

He was leaning back against the draining-board and his eyes had a dark and fathomless look that was so infinitely disturbing she shivered. She held his gaze for as long as she was able to and somehow, although her hands were horribly unsteady and her heart pounded hard enough to fill her head like a drum-beat, she managed to sound surprisingly confident.

'I know your opinion of me,' she said, 'and I think that does away with the need to lock my door. Now if you'll let me get on with the washing-up——'

Rather surprisingly Manuel said nothing at all, but he continued to look at her for several moments with his eyes slightly narrowed and a curious air of stillness about him. Then he walked past her suddenly, brushing against her as he did so and jolting her pulse into violent response once more. When she heard the door close behind him she heaved a great sigh, but she couldn't have said whether it was a sigh of relief or regret. Only the coming night would show whether or not she should have taken it all more seriously.

CHAPTER SEVEN

IT had taken Kristie a long time to get off to sleep because, although she had denied there was any need for her to be concerned about her situation, she had found herself lying there listening to the endless whispering of the wind and imagining she could hear footsteps coming along the corridor outside her bedroom door. She told herself that not for a minute did she believe Manuel would come to her room, and if he did she was perfectly capable of coping. Yet deep in her heart she knew that her will-power would wilt as it always did before that virile arrogance of his, so she had lain for hours, listening and letting her imagination run riot.

Inevitably when she did get to sleep she slept deeply and for a lot longer than she normally did. When she woke the sun was already well risen and running in long golden streaks across her bedroom floor, and she felt the beginnings of her always healthy appetite urging her to get up. She had no idea what time breakfast was expected to be ready, but in the circumstances she had no intention of putting herself out too much, so she took her time bathing and dressing.

She took rather more trouble over her appearance too, although if anyone had suggested it she would have denied it indignantly, nevertheless she chose which dress to wear with more than ordinary care, even though she had only three to choose from. A pale yellow one with brief sleeves and a full skirt did more for her than either of the other two, so she put that on, then stood for a moment or two smoothing down the skirt while she looked at herself in the mirror.

It didn't really matter how she looked, she told herself as she stood there idly appreciating the effect of pale yellow with her black hair and pale skin, Manuel wasn't going to be impressed. He was forewarned against what he called her tricks, and therefore presumably forearmed, yet she still couldn't resist making the most of her appearance.

At some time during those long wakeful hours last night, she had faced the fact that when she went and hid herself in the tower room rather than be taken back to Seville, she had no real idea of what she hoped to achieve. Yet as the situation had evolved there were certain aspects of it that made her think the ruse had not been entirely unsuccessful, and there was still the whole of Sunday before her yet.

As she made her way downstairs a few minutes later there was a curious churning sensation in her stomach that she found hard to account for; except that now that she was about to see him again she was suddenly even more conscious of their complete isolation. Even more than she had been last night during those long wakeful hours.

As she walked across the hall the smell of fresh coffee made her wrinkle her nose appreciatively even while she puzzled over it. It was possible, she supposed, that José had been concerned enough about his employer's plight to come back and see how he was doing. But if anyone had arrived by car she could almost guarantee that Manuel's first thought would not have been of breakfast, but of getting back to Seville as soon as possible, and the aroma of coffee could therefore mean only one thing.

Because she had imagined him far too chauvinistic to even know how to begin to make coffee, she stared as she opened the kitchen door and saw Manuel sitting there. He was wearing a brown shirt that made a stunning contrast to his famous golden colouring, and he looked completely at ease, sitting at the kitchen table and pouring himself coffee from José's big earthenware pot; coffee that he must have made himself because there was no one else there.

When she opened the door he looked up and half smiled, then held up the pot of coffee invitingly. 'Good morning,' he said and, catching her brief nod, inclined his head towards the row of cups hanging on the dresser behind him. 'Get yourself a cup.'

Still too taken aback for a moment to say anything, Kristie did as he said and got herself a cup, coping with a quite unexpected situation. She had half expected him to be indignant if he had been waiting for his breakfast, instead of which he seemed mildly amiable. 'You made the coffee?' she asked, and a raised brow took note of her surprise.

'It's the limit of my culinary skill,' he warned her, 'the rest is up to you. I don't know where anything else is kept.'

'How very convenient!'

The jibe wasn't made entirely in jest, but she smiled when she said it, and from the way he looked Manuel didn't take it amiss. 'I've done my part,' he said. 'Kitchen duties are yours, but I needed a cup of coffee, and you seemed to be sleeping late.'

'Not really late,' Kristie argued mildly. 'I just overslept a little, that's all.'

She had no intention of exchanging insults with him this early in the day, and she allowed herself to be drawn no further, but set about finding something for their breakfast. José kept part-baked rolls on hand for emergencies, she knew, and she took a packet from his well-stocked fridge and put them on to a baking tray while Manuel sat watching her and drinking his coffee, seemingly well content with the situation.

Only when the rolls were cooking and she had put the table ready did she again give him her attention, leaning against the edge of the table with her own cup in her hand. 'This is a new departure for you, isn't it?' she asked, and gave him a look that wasn't entirely without provocation and she would have been the first to admit. 'I hadn't seen you as the type to eat in the kitchen.'

Manuel was sitting as he so often did, with his elbows resting on the table and his coffee cup clasped between his hands, and looking at her with that steady, enigmatic gaze she always found so disturbing. 'Nor had I imagined you to be domesticated,' he remarked with a lift of one brow, 'but you've proved yourself an excellent cook. Although I suspect you've had very little more practice than I have at eating in kitchens.'

It was inevitable he should score off her, Kristie thought ruefully, and admitted her own shortcomings with a slight grimace. 'I don't profess to be domesticated,' she allowed, 'and if I'm a good cook it must be only what I've picked up from watching Aunt Maria or my mother. On the other hand, maybe I have a gift for it, who knows?'

'Who knows?' Manuel echoed with a faint smile. He pulled out the chair next to his at the table and patted the seat. 'Sit down and drink your coffee, the rolls won't be ready yet.' Although she did as he said, to Kristie there was something almost dangerously intimate about breakfasting in the kitchen with him, and she again felt that curious sense of anticipation in her stomach. Hastily switching her gaze when he caught her eye, she thought his look was faintly mocking. 'Did you sleep well?' he asked, and her heart lurched warningly as she nodded. 'No—anxious moments?'

Almost as if he knew how long she had lain last night, listening. 'None at all!' she denied firmly.

'That's good.'

He spoke so softly that it seemed to Kristie he used that disturbing voice of his quite deliberately for effect, and she rued the colour that warmed her cheeks because she knew he was bound to notice it as he always did. It was never easy to judge his mood and she found it more difficult than usual this morning, so that she kept her eyes averted because she knew he was still watching her.

It took only a few minutes for the rolls to cook, and having to keep an eye on them was an excellent opportunity to busy herself instead of sitting there being scrutinised. Manuel was a disconcerting table companion at any time, and in the present circumstances his earthy virility had never been more apparent, nor her own weakness where he was concerned.

It was for that reason that she endeavoured to keep the conversation off the matter of their present isolation and talked instead about the old castle and its history—a subject on which he seemed surprisingly willing to be drawn. 'You must know every inch of it,' she suggested, but Manuel pursed his lips dubiously.

'Not quite,' he demurred. 'I went all over it before I bought it, of course, but I've never found time to really get to know it. I'm not even sure how many rooms there are, except that there are far too many for my use, and none of them are habitable except the ones in use every day. But its position, its isolation, suits me perfectly and I've never had cause to regret buying it; it was something——'

He finished the sentence with a shrug, but something about the way he spoke made her suspect he had a very definite attachment to the old castle. 'You wouldn't part with it?' she said, and noticed his slight frown at the suggestion.

'Never!' he said firmly.

It would probably have surprised him to learn that Kristie had a strong streak of sentiment in her make-up, but nevertheless it was true, and she found it rather sad to think that such a once magnificent stronghold had become little more than an office. With an elbow resting on the table and her chin on her hand, her eyes had a vaguely far-away look for a moment as she visualised it as it might once have been, full of colour and sound and dark Moorish faces.

'It seems such a shame that it's empty,' she remarked. 'It must have been really magnificent once upon a time and now it's like a ghost. Even the fountain isn't working, and the gardens are gone; it's rather sad.'

'You think I should open it all up and take in tourists?' From his voice the very idea appalled him, and it startled Kristie for a moment when she looked at him to see amusement in his eyes instead of dislike.

'Of course you couldn't do that in the circumstances,' she said, and looked at him with a hint of reproach because she felt sure he was laughing at her. 'All I'm saying is that it seems a shame it's so—neglected. I remember when I came up here in the car and saw it for the first time, it reminded me of something out of a legend, with all those turrets, and suspended above that huge chasm.'

'The sort of place where the villain keeps the beautiful heroine locked up in a tower and has his wicked way with her?' Manuel suggested softly, and now there was not only amusement in his eyes but something else that brought swift, hot colour to her cheeks.

'The original owners very likely did just that,' she said in a quick, light voice, 'but women are better able to look after themselves these days. The villain would probably find himself hurled over the parapet into the chasm!'

'Ah yes, you'd find that more practical than waiting to be rescued by the handsome hero, of course,' Manuel observed dryly, and Kristie found herself taking him seriously enough to shake her head without a suggestion of a smile.

'A place like this, once that great door was closed, would be impregnable,' she insisted. 'Not even the most determined hero could get in; the wretched girl would have to cope on her own.'

She noted his faint smile uneasily. 'How wise of you to realise it,' he said and, because she felt things were getting much too personal for comfort, Kristie took steps to end it.

Getting up from the table, she started to gather the breakfast things together on to a tray. 'Whatever the whys and wherefores of it,' she said, 'I've got more practical things to do, like washing up and deciding what we're going to eat for the rest of the day.'

'There's plenty of food?'

It seemed to Kristie that he sounded vaguely anxious about it, and just for a moment she was tempted to lead him on. Eventually, however, she opened the door of the large modern freezer and showed him the contents, her eyes mocking him because it was so seldom she had the upper hand. 'José's a good housekeeper,' she told him.

'You won't go hungry, don't worry.'

She half expected some kind of retort from him, but a brief glance from the corner of her eye suggested he was thinking about something else. She didn't expect him to offer to dry the dishes, for she doubted if it would even occur to him, but he *had* made the coffee, and Kristie supposed that was as much help as she could expect from a man like Manuel.

'Just how genuinely interested are you in the castle and its history?'

She half turned her head and frowned at him curiously. 'I'm very interested,' she assured him. 'For one thing because I can't imagine anything more exciting than owning your own castle, and as I'm never likely to have one of my own, being able to admire someone else's is the next best thing.'

'Then you'd like to see the rest of it?'

Kristie had no hesitation; she would love to see the rest of it and said so. 'Oh, but of course I would!'

'There are dozens of rooms, all of them empty.'

He might have been trying to put her off, but Kristie didn't think so, and she wouldn't be put off anyway. 'Of course there are,' she said. 'That's half the fun of castles, isn't it? Having so many rooms that you can get lost in them.'

'And I dare say there are mice, possibly even rats,' Manuel insisted, and again Kristie looked over her shoulder at him as she put the last cup through the suds.

It was very hard to know what exactly was going on behind that steady, enigmatic gaze, for his expression gave nothing away, yet her heart began a harder, faster beat suddenly and that little curl of anticipation fluttered in her stomach again as she reached for a tea-towel. 'Just as long as there aren't any bats,' she said. 'I have a horror of bats, although I can't think why, they're a lot less harmful than rats.'

'But they have a reputation for haunting old castles,' Manuel reminded her, and once more he seemed faintly amused by her confession. 'There shouldn't be any about at this time of day, so you'd be safe enough.'

'Then I've nothing to worry about.' She couldn't be mistaken, Kristie felt sure. He was telling her in a rather roundabout way that she could explore the rest of the castle if she wanted to, and she didn't believe he meant her to go alone, although she didn't take too much for granted as yet. 'If I have your permission, I'll go on a tour of inspection as soon as I've finished the washing-up, and if I come across any bats I'll yell for help.'

'I was proposing to come with you,' Manuel told her quietly, and the softness of his voice slid like a finger along her spine. 'Unless, of course, you'd rather go alone.'

She would have been bitterly disappointed if he hadn't wanted to accompany her, Kristie realised, and she hastily decried any suggestion that she would rather go alone. 'Oh no, not at all!' Turning to face him while she dried her hands, she felt strangely shy suddenly and shook her head, once more avoiding that steady, disconcerting gaze as he got to his feet. 'I—I just didn't know if you wanted to, that's all. I mean, I wasn't sure just how much of an enthusiast you are.'

'Maybe,' Manuel observed with a touch of dryness, 'you're learning more about me by not trying so hard.'

The same thought crossed Kristie's mind some time later when they walked into yet another of the vast and seemingly endless rooms. The windows in this instance looked down over a steep, maquis-covered mountainside, warmly scented in the growing heat of the sun, and beyond it a landscape of mountains and sky. Even his earlier conversation had not made it clear just how great his knowledge and interest were, and he had kept her enthralled during their leisurely progress.

Kristie had never before heard him talk at such length or so enthusiastically about anything, and the animation and warmth of feeling in his face was a revelation. So that as he stood beside her, looking out at the vast, rolling miles of mountain scenery it gave her a curious thrill to recall how completely isolated they were. Just the two of them in that romantic old castle.

The thought of risk had never entered her head when she impulsively decided to make herself scarce instead of going back to Seville when she was supposed to. Only now did she stop to consider the awful loneliness she would have known if Manuel hadn't bothered to remain with her, and she shuddered involuntarily.

They stood framed in the high stone arch of one of the windows, and Manuel half turned to face her when he noticed the slight quiver of her body. 'What's the matter? You shuddered.' He reached and lightly touched her cheek with a fingertip, his eyes quizzical, and Kristie shook her head.

'It was nothing, just someone walking over my grave,' she said, but obviously Manuel had never heard the saying and he frowned over it.

'That's a curious thing to say—what does it mean?'

She shrugged, looking out of the window again rather than at him. 'Oh, it's a saying we have in England. When an unexpected shiver catches you unaware, we say someone just walked over your grave.'

'I live and learn!'

He went on facing her, leaning back against the stone window arch, and his eyes were heavy-lidded and half hidden, but they affected her strangely for all that. No matter how much they argued, or how much she despaired of her own weakness, he could affect her as no man had ever done before, and knowing how completely alone they were, her heart beat almost chokingly hard.

'Tell me some more about Castillo Cuchicheo,' she said, and her voice vied with the wind in its whispering softness. 'You must have gone into its history very thoroughly to know so much about it.'

Manuel didn't reply immediately, instead he turned his head and once more looked out at the hot, lonely countryside. 'I heard the legends of Castillo Cuchicheo like most children hear fairy stories,' he said, 'and I never tired of hearing them even after I grew older. Right up until about fifty years ago the castle was in the hands of the same family for several hundred years, and it was from one of that same family that I learned all about it. He, like his father before him, always hoped to bring it back into the family.'

'But instead you got it.'

'I got it,' Manuel agreed, and his eyes were broodingly sombre between their thick lashes, 'and he never knew.'

Kristie looked at him from the corner of her eye, for she felt strangely close to him, as if, just for a moment, she had managed to breach that wall he put between himself and the rest of the world. 'Was he a friend?' she asked. 'Or a relative, maybe?'

Once more he was a long time answering, so long, in fact, that Kristie began to feel as if he had forgotten she was even there. He watched the distant mountain peaks as if they hypnotised him, and there was a strange, haunted look on his face that made him appear much older. If she had managed to get through his barrier of secrecy a few moments ago, she was now very firmly excluded, it seemed, and it gave her a curious sense of loneliness as she stood beside him, so that eventually she reached out and lightly touched his arm.

At once he turned back to her, frowning slightly, as if he resented her breaking into his brooding silence, then he shook his head quickly and dismissively. 'He was a friend,' he told her, obviously bringing himself back to earth. 'He was also my stepfather—Don Alonso de Mena.'

Recalling his earlier reference, she made the next enquiry very tentatively. 'He—he died before you got the castle?'

Manuel's brows were drawn close and his mouth tight set. 'He died,' he confirmed in a flat hard voice, 'and I wasn't there to tell him how much he meant to me.'

Whatever the cause of his stepfather's death, it had obviously affected him deeply, and it was hard to know what to say. The helpless spread of her hands was as Spanish as anything she ever did and expressed everything she felt. 'I'm sorry,' she said.

In fact the very simplicity of the statement seemed to

have the effect of restoring normality, and Manuel heaved himself away from the window arch and stood for a moment looking down at her, then a faint smile touched his firm mouth briefly. 'Didn't I say that you learned more about me by not trying?' he said. 'You have a gift for listening and letting people talk that must be quite an asset in your business.'

After the last few hours of more or less peaceful coexistence the remark struck Kristie like a blow in the face, and she shook her head in reproach while a swift tongue passed across her lips. 'Was that just too much to resist?' she asked huskily. 'I can't think even you believe I'd make use of anything you tell me in—in these circumstances.'

But he very likely did believe it, she realised bitterly, it was exactly what he would expect of her. And not only Manuel but her editor too, would expect her to make the most of any scrap of information she learned about him. It was, after all, the first real break-through into his personal life and she had not even had to probe very hard for it, but she was very reluctant to follow up in her professional capacity.

'But isn't it what you're paid for?' Manuel asked, and Kristie curved her hands tightly over the edge of the window as she leaned her head out, her lips tremblingly unsteady.

Below her the soft, muted colours of the maquis added their scent to the hot, dry air, and because of the castle's position on a hilltop, a bird flew almost level with the window, soaring up into the harsh blueness of the sky. She should have felt resentful, yet there was a curious lightness in her heart despite the brief hurt he had inflicted, and after a moment she turned her head and looked at him. Her eyes were deeply blue and much more intent than she realised, but she said nothing to reproach him.

Her pulse quickened when he reached out and lightly touched her face, curving his long fingers about it, and bringing swift colour to her cheeks. 'I'm sorry,' he murmured and, because an apology was the very last thing she expected, Kristie shook her head.

'No, it's true,' she insisted urgently. 'It *is* what I'm paid for, and if I was anything like as good a journalist as I like to think I am I'd make the most of anything and everything; only——'

'You're not quite such a dedicated and hard-core newshound as you thought you were,' Manuel suggested softly.

Her laughter was instinctive, a light, shivery sound that barely stirred the stillness of the empty room. 'Obviously I'm not,' she said.

It was vaguely alarming to realise how close he was suddenly, and the warm touch of his body acted like a spark that kindled her all too responsive senses. Moving his hand round under her hair, he lifted it from her neck a little, stroking her skin with his long fingers until she felt little thrills all along her spine. Thick lashes concealed the expression in his eyes, but failed to disguise the unmistakable glow of passion as he looked down into her face.

'Obviously you're not,' he echoed.

With her head cradled in one hand, he slipped the other round to the small of her back and drew her towards him until the bold, hard virility of him fired her senses and she arched her body to meet his. Drawing her still closer, he held her so hard that she could scarcely breathe, yet still her body clamoured to be nearer and she reached up her arms to encircle his neck and twine her fingers into his hair.

'Kristie.'

He whispered her name, close to her lips so that his breath warmed her mouth and brought a soft, instinctive sigh from her. His lips pursed, he touched her cheeks and her half-closed eyes and the soft, scented skin beside her ears, then his hands moved upward, encircling her neck and slowly pushing the collar of her dress open. Long fingers flicked each button until the light material slid down her shoulders under his hands, and he kissed her neck and her throat, lightly and lingeringly.

When he bent his head to put his lips to her shoulder

Kristie turned her head with a soft moan of pleasure and kissed the firm warmth of his cheek, her lips pulsing with the same wild beat that seemed to fill her whole body, tingling with excitement and anticipation she had never dreamed of before.

Just briefly Manuel lifted his head and looked directly into her face and the searing heat of passion in those stunning amber eyes deprived her of every scrap of will-power. His mouth brushed hers lightly, seeking a response he must know she was bound to make, and then, when she parted her lips in breathless urgency, he buried his mouth in hers, arousing in her a desire as compelling and devastating as his own.

It was another world, a fiery, all-devouring world of passion and desire that lifted her to heights she had only dreamed of. And even though the wind still whispered from every corner of the vast room, and the fluttering shadow of the bird in its solitary flight fell briefly on to her upturned face as it crossed the sun, nothing roused her from that wild ecstasy, for her heart winged as freely as the bird's flight.

It took something as hard, sharp and unexpected as the crack of a rifle shot to bring her crashing back to reality, and her eyes were drawn irresistibly to the light puff of feathers plummeting downward past the window, and she stared at it in horror. Silent suddenly, and no longer graceful, the body of the bird plunged out of sight below the edge of the window, clumsy with the weight of death, and she clutched Manuel in sudden and inexplicable fear.

'Manuel!'

'It's all right, it's nothing.'

'It's dead!'

He pressed her close to him and his lips brushed her forehead, his voice tender and consoling, as if she was a child. 'People do come hunting in these mountains, little one, especially at weekends. The creature died quickly, you have no need to look so anguished.'

She was trembling and not entirely able to understand her own reaction, and Kristie clung to him with both hands, burying her face in the softness of his shirt. The suddenness of the bird's end had shocked her, but she couldn't explain it to him, even while he held her so close she could feel the hard, steady beat of his heart against her face.

One moment the creature had been soaring up into the sky with the same glorious abandon as her own heart, and the next it was limply dropping at the feet of its killer. The similitude was too close for her to accept Manuel's matter-of-fact assessment at once, and she went on clinging to him while he held her close, soothing his hands over her back.

When she eventually looked up at him it was with a hint of uncertainty, for she hardly expected him to understand how she felt. 'It—it was so—unexpected,' she whispered, not really excusing herself, although it might have sounded like it, and Manuel nodded. He ran his hands through her hair and there was still enticement in the light touch of his body against hers, so that it was hard for her to breathe without her breast heaving and her lips parting. But the moment of delirious ecstasy was shattered, and Kristie was already far enough back to earth to realise it. 'I thought we were alone up here,' she ventured, and Manuel touched the nape of her neck with his fingertips, making her shiver.

'There are no houses nearer than five kilometres,' he warned her. A slight roughness in his voice betrayed how easily that searing passion could be rekindled, and she steeled her heart against allowing it to. 'Our hunter most likely came up from the city.'

Her senses told her that he no more wanted to discuss the man, whoever he was, than she did herself, but Kristie felt the need suddenly to have both feet firmly on the ground. 'Whoever he is, I don't like him!' she declared, and turned her head to look out of the window once more.

It was the slight pressure of Manuel's hands on her neck that drew her attention back to him, although she didn't meet his eyes. 'Kristie?'

'Do you ever go out there and—kill things?' she asked, and again his hands pressed against her neck for a moment, as if he suspected she was accusing him.

'In the normal course of things, when I'm here I don't have time for hunting,' he reminded her quietly, and once more he ran his hands through the silky blackness of her hair before tipping her head back in the hope of making her look at him. 'Would it change your opinion of me if I did, Kristie?'

In her present state of mind Kristie couldn't be sure just what her opinion of him was, for it had undergone so many different changes during the past few days. She found him irresistibly attractive, she couldn't deny that, yet even after he had kissed her and she was lightheaded with the sheer exhilaration of it, something rang faint warning bells in the back of her mind, however hard she tried to ignore them.

Inevitably she knew he must have been in the same situation, done the same things, with other women, but it was a fact she found increasingly hard to accept. He hated publicity, it was true, but that did not necessarily mean that he lived like a monk and avoided women's company, and he was a skilled enough lover to suggest he had had a great deal of experience.

'Did you hear me, Kristie?'

He held her face cupped in his hands and looked down at her with a look in those stunning golden eyes that made her tremble, and when she looked away he used the pads of his thumbs to try and lift her lids again. 'I don't think I know what my opinion is,' she said, 'but I'm not really in favour of killing things for the mere pleasure of it.'

'You little Englishwoman!' he jibed softly, and bent for a moment to put his lips to hers.

'Oh, but it goes on in England too,' Kristie hastened to assure him, for she was always just as ready to defend her Spanish blood as her English, and anxious not to be beguiled again by the touch of his mouth. 'It's just a matter of opinion, I suppose.'

'And I never suspected you of having a tender heart!'

Laughter deepened and mellowed his voice and it would have been so easy to yield to the clamour of her senses, something she didn't want to happen. Not while she could tell herself he had played out this same situation with other women. She should accept it as inevitable, but it wasn't as easy to do as she wanted it to be, and she eased herself away from those gentle, persuasive hands as undemonstratively as she could.

Manuel was frowning, she sensed it as she turned to the window again, and when she smoothed down the skirt of her dress her hands were trembling. 'What is it, Kristie?'

The question was asked softly and in the tone of voice that could play such havoc with her common sense, so that she was shaking her head even while she answered him. 'Nothing really,' she denied, keeping her voice as steady as she could in the circumstances. 'It's just that—I have to keep reminding myself that we have this great place to ourselves.'

She felt rather a fraud, using that as an excuse, but as it happened it appeared to be one that Manuel was willing to accept. She was leaning on the window ledge and her hands gripped it tightly when he laid his hands on her shoulders briefly while he pressed a kiss on to her neck. 'Of course I understand,' he murmured close to her ear. 'I've misjudged you more than I realised, Kristie, and you don't know how sorry I am. This isn't quite what you imagined when you went and hid yourself yesterday morning, is it?' She shook her head rather than answer him and heard him sigh deeply, although she couldn't guess exactly what caused it. 'Your family will be worrying about you, even though I did explain, and that good-looking cousin of yours will be suspecting the very worst.'

'Juan?' She half turned her head, wondering what had prompted him to mention Juan. 'There's no more reason why Juan should suspect any more than Aunt Maria, and he certainly has no more right to take exception to what I do.' She looked at him directly for a moment, though it weakened her resistance alarmingly. 'I've told you before, Manuel, there's nothing like that between Juan and me.'

'Ah!'

Kristie would never have believed that so much satisfaction could have gone into a single syllable, and once more Manuel's lips brushed lightly across her neck. When, after a moment or two, she turned from the window with the obvious intention of going, he held out a hand and she put her own into it, thrilling to the warm pressure of his fingers as they clasped hers.

'I promise you you have nothing to worry about,' he said as they walked the width of the room, and Kristie looked up at him, not quite sure what he was trying to say to her. 'I shan't take advantage of having you here alone,' Manuel explained in the same quiet and reassuring voice. 'I may have harboured some pretty unflattering opinions of you, Kristie, but I think I've learned quite a bit about you in the past few hours, and I promise you can trust me from now on.'

It wasn't the kind of speech that Kristie expected from him, nor was it what she wanted to hear, she realised, but to tell him so would only convince him that he had yet again been fooled by appearances. With her eyes downcast, she waited while he closed the door behind them, then glanced up briefly and smiled.

'I *do* trust you,' she assured him in a small voice, and he squeezed her fingers lightly, pausing for a moment to look down at her.

'We seem to have changed roles to some extent, don't we?' he asked with a faint smile. 'You were so determined to find all you could about me, and instead I've discovered a completely different side to you.' He raised the hand he held and pressed it briefly to his lips. 'I like what I see much better than I did that determinedly bold harridan who chased me so relentlessly,' he murmured. 'Is this the real you, Kristie?'

'I—I think so.'

She had never felt less like a determined journalist on the track of a story as she stood there with the colour in her cheeks and her eyes downcast, and she realised with dismay that he had completely disarmed her. 'Then I shall want to find out more about you,' Manuel promised softly, and again he raised her hand briefly to his lips. 'But I'm a patient man, I can wait.'

She couldn't go on, Kristie knew. She couldn't carry on trying to discover what secret it was he kept hidden away in his heart, the reason he had left the limelight when he did. The story that could have made her name as a journalist had suddenly become less important than the man who now looked at her with his warm, amber eyes and touched every nerve in her body.

It was curious how much bigger and richer the Spanish moon seemed than the pale shimmering ghost that lit the skies at home, and Kristie smiled as she looked at it through her open window. It wasn't her habit to sleep with her bedroom window open, but somehow felt very different from her usual self tonight.

The mingled scents of the maquis drifted up to her as she settled back on the pillows, and she smiled, for it exactly fitted her mood. The rest of the day had passed like a dream. Manuel had complimented her cooking unstintingly, then smiled at the inevitable blushes, and while Kristie wished there was something she could do about it, Manuel was obviously delighted by it. Blushing was an old-fashioned virtue and as such he admired it.

He had kept his word and not even touched her since their morning tour of the castle, but quite obviously to a man like Manuel physical contact wasn't always necessary. There was the subtlety of a caress in his voice that could send thrills chasing one another along her spine, and never before had those amber-gold eyes been used with such devastating effect. She didn't want to fall in love with him, it didn't fit in with her plans at all, but as she drifted off into sleep it occurred to her that she might not be able to do anything about it.

It was some time in the early hours of the morning when she woke suddenly feeling as if her heart was about to burst out of her body, it was beating so hard. Yet she could see nothing and hear nothing to suggest a cause, and she lay for a moment as if petrified, trying to decide what could have woken her in such alarm.

The moon was no longer in sight, but it still lit up her room and she could discover nothing different from normal except the open window, and it was when she got out of bed to close it that she saw something that brought a sickening lurch of fear to her heart. She was part way across the floor when a small dark shadowy creature with crimped wings flew in through the window and came directly for her.

Her remark to Manuel about being frightened to death of bats had been no exaggeration, and even as the creature's sensitive antennae picked her up as an obstruction and it turned swiftly and flew out again, Kristie screamed. Not with the hope or intent of being heard, but from sheer animal instinct. She screamed again and even more loudly when another of the creatures flew in, coming directly for her just as before, and turning at the last moment to go skimming silently out into the night.

It was instinct too that sent her running out into the corridor, and just as she came out of her room Manuel emerged from his, tying the sash of a blue silk robe as he came running towards her. Without even asking what was wrong he took her into his arms and held her tightly, while Kristie clung to him for a moment in sheer relief.

It was only when he murmured enquiringly that she felt the first twinge of selfconsciousness for the fuss she had made, and preferred to go on hiding her face rather than look at him. 'What is it, Kristie?' he asked, his lips close to her ear. 'What on earth frightened you?'

Her heart was pumping hard and with her face pressed to his chest she could feel his heart too; steadier than her own, but faster than usual. His arms were completely around her, holding her firm, and the slight pressure of his hands on her breast did little to settle her pulse, but instead roused it to a more erratic beat, and she had no desire to be anywhere at the moment but close in his arms with his face resting on the soft dishevelment of her hair.

'Kristie?' He held her away from him at last, though he still kept his arms around her, looking down at her with gentle, enquiring eyes. 'What is it, little one, eh?'

Kristie met his eyes for only a moment, then looked away again, and there was a flush of colour in her face when she told him. 'Bats,' she said in a small quivery voice. 'There were two of them in my room. I know I'm a terrible coward, but they scared the life out of me and I—well, I just screamed.'

Manuel did not relinquish his protective hold on her, even now that he knew there was no actual danger, but there was a little glimmer of amusement in his eyes which, in view of the hour and the fact that he must have been woken from sleep, was quite unexpected. He raised one brow quizzically. 'Do you want me to come and chase them out for you?' he asked softly, and Kristie nodded without speaking.

Still keeping one arm around her, he walked into her bedroom, and immediately she was reminded of the last time he was there. Surely this time he wouldn't suspect her motives; not at one o'clock in the morning. As they went in he looked around the dim, moonlit room, and it was only then that Kristie realised she hadn't even put the light on.

Reaching back, he switched on the overhead light, but nothing stirred, only the slight whisper of the curtains in the wind, and Kristie's eyes were drawn to the gaping darkness of the open window. Either her screams had scared the creatures off or they had abandoned their hunting in that particular spot, for there was no sign of them, and Manuel looked down at her and arched one brow.

'They *were* here,' she insisted huskily. 'One after the other, they came in and flew straight out again; maybe I scared them off when I screamed.'

'There was probably only one,' Manuel informed her, and sounded very much as if he knew what he was talking about. 'They follow a flight path looking for food and with your window open there was nothing to tell the thing it wasn't on a continuous route. It would turn when it picked up the solid wall on the other side of the room; more than likely it's given up now.'

Not altogether reassured, Kristie eyed the open window anxiously. 'I'd rather the window was closed,' she told him, 'Just in case it comes back.'

'Yes, of course.'

He left her to go and close the window, but she felt a prickle of resentment for the glint of amusement in his eyes as he glanced at her before he moved away. Standing in the middle of the room, she felt suddenly rather bereft without his arm around her, and as she watched his tall, lean figure go striding across the room she could do nothing about the more urgent beat of her heart, and the irrepressible flutter of excitement she felt.

'I suppose you think I'm a terrible coward for making so much fuss,' she ventured defensively, but Manuel made no reply until he had pulled the window shut and carefully fastened it.

Then he turned around and stood for a moment with both hands thrust into the pockets of his robe, his eyes shadowed by their lashes, and looking as enigmatic as she had ever seen him. 'I don't think so at all,' he said. 'It was a very feminine reaction.' And with his hidebound ideas about women he wouldn't take it as much amiss as if she'd dealt with the wretched creature herself, Kristie thought dryly. 'But what woke you up in the first place, Kristie?'

He stayed where he was, across the far side of the room, and nothing would convince Kristie that he wasn't deliberately keeping his distance now that the immediate panic was over. She could feel herself trembling, and for the first time realised that she hadn't stopped to put on a robe when she ran out of the room. Her nightgown was a flimsy pale blue and only the folds of it screened her body as she stood with her hands clasping her arms, flushed and alarmingly selfconscious.

'I—I don't know,' she confessed. 'I don't usually leave my window open and I suppose it was—it was some kind of—instinct that made me wake up. I know they're harmless,' she went on swiftly, 'but I've always had a horror of them, and when it came in the window and made straight for me I—I panicked.'

Manuel still remained where he was, keeping half the width of the room between them, and he said nothing for a moment, then inclined his head slightly towards the bed. 'You'd better get back into bed,' he said quietly.

Kristie didn't argue, she didn't even hesitate, but slipped quickly across the room and into bed, pulling the bedclothes up around her waist and sitting with her hands curved over the edge of them. 'I—I'm grateful to you,' she whispered, and noticed that he smiled faintly.

'I closed the window,' he observed in that devastatingly quiet voice, 'that's all.'

Kristie could only think of the warmth and strength of his arms around her, and the pulsing steadiness of his heartbeat against her cheek, and when he looked at her something in those glowing amber eyes touched her like a physical caress. From the flushed uncertainty of her face they moved slowly on down over her bare shoulders to the thin, pale scar on her left breast, and no caressing hand could have aroused her senses more, or brought a more urgent need of his nearness.

'With the window closed you won't be troubled any more,' he said, and even the tone of his voice slid like light, caressing fingers along her spine.

Kristie met his eyes for a brief moment and the hot fierce passion that burned there brought an almost inaudible sigh from her as she half closed her eyes. Her body pulsed with life, throbbing with the desire to be held close to him, and the slow sweep of his tongue across his lips aroused an agonising need for his kiss.

'Oh, Holy Mother!'

Kristie knew exactly what kind of temptation had brought that moan of agony from him, for she would have given anything for him to come to her, and her voice had the same kind of huskiness. 'Manuel——'

It wasn't an invitation, it was an appeal, and her eyes

glowed like blue jewels between their black lashes. She was trembling like a leaf because she knew that if he came even a step nearer resistance would crumble. A hand on her arm, or the lightest brush of his lips, would be enough to fire more passionate needs, and he had sworn not to take advantage of their isolation. Clutching tightly to the edge of the bedclothes, Kristie prayed he wouldn't come because he would never believe in her again if she allowed him into her bed, and if he came she knew she hadn't the strength of will to turn him away.

'Goodnight, Kristie!'

The words were murmured in a huskily deep voice and for a moment they barely registered in her dazed brain as she watched his tall, striding figure making for the open door. He didn't turn and look at her again, and Kristie quickly moistened her lips with the tip of her tongue, her words just reaching him before he flicked off the overhead light and plunged her into darkness.

'Goodnight,' she whispered, torn between relief and disappointment as the door closed softly behind him.

CHAPTER EIGHT

Iᴛ was fairly late the following morning when Kristie woke, but still she took a moment or two longer to consider her position. Last night Manuel had been very determined to stick by his vow not to take advantage of his position, and even this morning Kristie wasn't entirely sure how she felt about his strength of will. Everything was so very different from what she had expected when she hid herself away rather than go back to Seville, but whatever else she felt, she knew that she wouldn't have exchanged this weekend alone with Manuel for anything.

It was Monday morning and José was due back, although not for a while yet, and that was something else that she had to consider. Nothing had been said about her going back with the chauffeur, Esteban, when he took the car back to Seville, and she hoped Manuel was going to let her stay on as his temporary secretary. Although nothing was further from her mind at the moment than the mundane duties of a secretary.

All the time she was bathing and dressing her mind returned again and again to her feelings for Manuel, and each time she turned hastily from the almost certain fact that she was dangerously close to being in love with him. He was the most intriguing and sensually attractive man she had ever known in her life, but she could see little hope of a future with him. Being in his arms yesterday had made her realise that things could never be quite the same for her again, but at the same time she dared not let herself fall too much in love with him.

As she went downstairs her legs felt alarmingly unsteady, and once again that curious little flutter of anticipation curled in her stomach, more noticeable than ever this morning. Just as she had the day before she wrinkled her nose as she came down into the hall, but this morning the smell wasn't of fresh-made coffee, but something sweeter and much more delicate, so that she frowned curiously.

Another thing she noticed too was the unmistakable splash and tinkle of water somewhere outside, and immediately she changed direction and made for the outer door. It was heavy and she opened it just a fraction, enough to be able to peer around the edge of it, then with a cry of surprise she flung it wide and stood for a moment looking out at the normally grey and deserted courtyard.

This morning it wasn't lifeless as she had so often complained it was, but brimming with life and colour. The big fountain was working and four rather battered stone lions spouted clear mountain water from their mouths, while a tall central jet leaped upwards, catching the sun and showering a myriad rainbow drops into the wide stone basin. Not only that, the basin itself overflowed around its perimeter with a mass of colourful blooms; armsful of them sprinkled with shimmering drops of spray, and more massed around under the rim—a dizzying riot of scent and colour that made it hard to believe it was nothing more than brush from the mountainside.

Kristie simply stood there for several moments, dazzled and delighted and misty-eyed with emotion, not only at the sight of the fountain and the blossoms, but at the thought of the gesture that had created it. It could only have been Manuel, and he had done it to please her, so how could she feel otherwise? Pleasure bubbled up inside her, warming her cheeks and giving a jewel brightness to her eyes as she walked out into the sunshine and revelled in the bright, earthy garden he had made for her, and she bent and buried her face in the cool mass of plants.

'Oh, Manuel!'

She whispered as she stroked her hands over the brushy scent of wild thyme and there was no longer any doubt in her heart. How could she not love a man who did such a thing to please her? Breaking off a sprig of wild thyme she held it to her nose while, for the sheer pleasure of it, she dabbled her fingers under the falling spray.

The whisper of sound she heard from inside the castle was barely audible above the sound of the fountain, but it was enough, and Kristie turned quickly. Manuel was standing just inside the hall watching her, and the glowing warmth of his eyes again aroused all those same urgent longings which this time were mingled with an indescribable tenderness.

Her laughter was for the sheer joy of seeing him and she went hurrying over to join him, looking up at him for a moment with the pleasure she felt written clear on her face. It was impulse alone that made her forget his vow of restraint, and she tiptoed to kiss his mouth with the sprig of wild thyme crushed between them, enveloping them in its rich, pungent scent.

'Thank you,' she whispered, her lips lingering on that firm, warm mouth. 'It's beautiful; it's the most beautiful garden I've ever seen, and you must have been up very early to gather all that maquis.'

'I'm glad you're pleased.' He didn't put his arms around her, although it was clear from the look in his eyes that that was what he wanted to do. and Kristie had never regretted that vow of his more than she did at that moment. 'You complained that it was dead and ghostly,' Manuel went on, 'and as there was no shortage of material to hand I did my best to remedy the fact. I know you find the brush flowers attractive as I do, and I could think of no other garden I could create so quickly; it was a spur-of-the-moment impulse, you see.' His eyes teased her gently. 'It must be something I've picked up from knowing you, for I was never impulsive that I remember.'

'Never?' she enquired, and heaven knew why she thought of his sudden and dramatic decision to withdraw from public life when she said it.

'Very seldom,' Manuel insisted.

She felt so glowingly content with the way things were that she smiled up at him. 'Well, I couldn't be more pleased that you were impulsive in this instance,' she told him in a slightly unsteady voice. 'I love my garden, but most of all I love the thought that went into making it.'

'I wasn't even sure if the fountain would work after all this time,' Manuel said. 'But Moorish workmanship is obviously every bit as good as it's reputed to be because only minutes after I turned it on, it began to flow.'

Kristie held out a hand to him and led him out into the courtyard, then she leaned forward and held both her hands under the sparkling spray that fell from the jet. 'Doesn't it make it come alive?' she insisted, trying to make him admit how worthwhile his efforts had been, and Manuel was half smiling, mocking her enthusiasm yet pleased by it at the same time.

'It does. And now I suppose I shall be expected to employ gardeners to establish a real garden.'

'It *would* be lovely!' Her eyes glowed as she visualised the huge and overgrown gardens alive with beds and borders of flowers and scented shrubs, a riot of colour and perfumes, softening the harsh outlines of the castle and giving it life and beauty. 'The gardens must have been beautiful once upon a time.'

'Your fairy-tale again,' Manuel mocked gently, but there was a more sombre look in his eyes, she noted, and he stroked a hand over the bristly tops of the plants as if his thoughts where elsewhere. 'It was one of the things my stepfather always said he would do when he got the castle back,' he said, and Kristie's heart gave a sudden lurch of surprise. Only once before had he mentioned anything about his family, and she felt as she had then, that he had somehow drifted away from her. 'He was a keen gardener,' Manuel was saying, 'and he loved to create beauty around him. The gardens at the Villa de Naranjos are his work, and I meant him to recreate these in time—only there *was* no time.'

'He didn't even know you'd bought the castle?' Kristie ventured softly, and he shook his head.

'It was meant to be a surprise. I was going to tell him the next time I went home, when all the negotiations had been completed and there was no chance of anything going wrong, but it was too late.'

She looked up at him again and noticed how much

older his features appeared, and her need to reach out and touch him was almost irresistible. 'Was—was he ill for long?'

'For years before he died,' said Manuel, 'that was why——'

He was shaking his head as if he found it too hard to talk about it, and purely on impulse Kristie laid a hand on his arm, looking up at him with compassion in her eyes. Her heart was thudding hard in her breast because some inner conviction made her believe she was about to learn the reason for the Golden Spaniard's sudden retirement, yet the idea of making capital out of it did not even enter her head.

'Whenever I was anywhere near home I went to see him,' Manuel was saying, and it seemed to Kristie that he spoke to himself rather than to her. 'He enjoyed my success and followed my career avidly, because it was he who encouraged me to take up the sport in the first place. From the time I was a little boy he encouraged me, and he was wild with joy the first time I won a race, teasing my mother because she was afraid for me.

'Then, at the height of the season three years ago, I received a message from my mother telling me that Papa was dying and had only a few more weeks to live. I wanted to go to him immediately, I almost did, and I agonised over it for hours, but the event was an important one and if I won it it would be the crowning achievement of my career. Also my mother had said he had weeks, and the event was only hours ahead, so I could take him the news of my victory and perhaps he would die a little happier for knowing. I just didn't believe I didn't have time to take part and still get home in time to be with him when he died.' He ran a hand through the thick red-gold hair at the side of his head, and the agony he felt showed in the stiff curve of his fingers. 'By the time I got there he had been dead for only a few hours—the hours I'd delayed so that I could win that last important event.'

'And you've never raced since,' Kristie whispered, her voice husky with emotion. 'Oh, Manuel, you had no need to punish yourself so harshly, he would have understood.'

Manuel said nothing for a while, but she noticed that gradually he was relaxing, as if the telling of it had fulfilled some need in him. Eventually he shook his head and once more ran a hand through his hair. 'You're saying almost exactly what Mama said to me,' he told her, and when he looked at her again it was clear that the tension had eased, and his eyes were less broodingly sombre. 'I still cannot believe that either of you are right, but it helps to hear it said, and as I've already told you, you have a talent for listening and drawing people out, Kristie.'

'I—I hope it helped to talk about it.'

'It did. Maybe we're all of us looking for someone to absolve us from our consciences, hmm?'

The most satisfying thing about it, Kristie found, was that he seemed not to even consider the possibility of her making use of what she had learned, and she leaned to press her face against the scented harshness of the maquis that clustered around the fountain's rim. How far she had come since those first uneasy days with him.

'I didn't realise how much you'd appreciate your garden.' The quietness of his voice made her look up, and when he smiled her heart clamoured like a wild thing in her breast. 'Are you a country girl at heart, Kristie? Is that your secret?'

She raised her face from the scented brush, knowing her cheeks were flushed, but for once uncaring. 'I think it must be,' she allowed in a small husky voice. 'I can't imagine anything more peaceful than living here in the mountains.'

'And gathering armsful of maquis?' he teased. 'You'd soon become bored, Kristie. Without your friends and your shopping expeditions, you'd be weeping with boredom in a month!'

'No, I wouldn't!'

Heaven knew why she was bothering to object so vehemently, for he could hardly be serious about it, since the question didn't even arise, but those incredible amber eyes could quicken her pulse without even a suggestion of physical contact. Just the same she wished he would put his arms around her, for she ached for the strength of his arms and the passionate fierceness of his mouth on hers.

But if Manuel felt the same urgent need, he resisted it, and his hands remained at his sides though his mouth pursed slightly, suggesting he too had kissing in mind. It was because she was trembling so much and finding it hard to think about anything but having him love her that she sought some kind of distraction. Something that would take her mind off matters that could could only make her situation more complicated when it came to the final showdown.

'You've done all this for me,' she said, and laughed huskily, 'and I haven't even begun to make breakfast for you. Are you very hungry?'

'I've been roaming around on the mountainside since just after seven,' Manuel told her with a glint of laughter in his eyes. 'Yes, my pigeon, I *am*—very hungry!'

The unexpected endearment sent her pulse soaring and her heart skipped as she quickly avoided his eyes. She stepped past him and walked back into the hall. 'Then I'd better do something about it,' she told him.

'I could wait for José to arrive and let him make breakfast,' Manuel said quietly, and she paused part-way across the hall and half turned, not quite sure of his intention.

'Is that what you'd rather do?' she asked, and with a faint smile, he shook his head.

One part of her hoped he would go and wait in the *salón* for his breakfast, but the other half of her wanted to spend as much time as possible with him before José returned. Since he had confided in her, out there by the fountain, she felt their relationship had undergone a change, and that it was much more close and intimate than before. Yet she was still strangely wary of him in some ways, almost as if she expected a sudden change in him; a reversion to his earlier suspicion.

He followed her into the kitchen and sat himself on the edge of the table, watching her put on the coffee and set rolls on a baking-sheet, and when instinct made her glance up at him suddenly, she noticed he was smiling; a curious and secret little smile that at any other time she would have questioned the meaning of. 'I like to see you domesticated,' he said, and the depth and softness of his voice skimmed along her spine. 'Doesn't it appeal to you at least as much as reporting, Kristie?'

'I—I don't know. It depends.'

'On what?' he asked with gentle insistence, and the effect of it was to make her unsteady hands let two of the rolls slide off the baking tray and on to the floor. It did nothing to help when Manuel bent to retrieve them at the same time as she did herself, and his long fingers closed, seemingly by accident, over hers. Then she looked up directly into those disturbing eyes again.

'No woman enjoys being domesticated with a man in her kitchen,' she told him, 'especially an amateur like me. It makes me nervous.'

'I'm sorry.' His hand still held hers and Kristie despaired of her own weakness. 'Would you rather I went away and left you?' he suggested softly, and she automatically shook her head.

Of course she wouldn't rather he went and left her, for there was very little time left when they could be alone, but on the other hand she wasn't going to make a very good job of getting breakfast if he stayed. 'It might be a better idea if I'm going to make any sort of success of getting breakfast for you,' she told him, and he looked at her with sombre eyes.

'And I *have* made a promise, eh?'

Kristie didn't reply, but there was nothing she could do until he took away his hand, and he did that only very slowly so that his long fingers stroked over her skin. They straightened up at the same moment, and he slipped a hand under her arm quite automatically, but that first light touch was enough, and she offered no resistance when he took the rolls from her hand and put them down on the table.

Standing with her eyes down cast, she breathed so

deeply that her breast rose and fell with exaggerated urgency, and she was trembling so much she wondered how she still managed to stand. Manuel stood close beside her, too close, for the pulsing virility of him affected her senses and made her head spin, and the amber eyes watched her with urgent intensity.

'I promised not to touch you again while we're here alone,' he whispered, 'but God help me, I can't help myself! Kristie!'

He slid both hands under her hair, resting the palms on the warmth of her neck, then drew her slowly towards him and touched her mouth with his. It was a light, seeking touch and Kristie raised her face to him in anticipation of a more passionate caress, and the sudden more hard pressure of his hands promised she would not be disappointed.

Nothing mattered to her but the fact that she was once more in his arms, and her senses responded to the sheer virile strength of him as she lifted her arms and clasped them around his neck. His hard masculinity was stunningly familiar as he drew her even closer and she offered her soft mouth, her lips parted, a willing offering to the fierceness of his kiss.

But it seemed he had scarcely touched her mouth than he raised his head suddenly and tilted it slightly to one side, as if he was listening. Startled, Kristie gazed up at him in bewildered surprise, and Manuel laughed softly as he bent to kiss her mouth again. 'José's back, my pigeon,' he murmured. 'You won't need to get breakfast after all, eh?'

Being so suddenly snatched back to reality, Kristie was too dazed for a moment to realise fully what he was telling her, but the moment she recognised footsteps in the hall, and Esteban's light friendly voice, she stepped back quickly and smoothed her shaking hands down her dress. Manuel had her face cupped in his hands and he brushed her lips with his before he spoke.

'José will never believe you can blush so enchantingly, my pigeon,' he whispered, and Kristie's eyes reproached him for bringing up the subject she was most sensitive about.

She wondered how one man could make such a difference in the span of a single weekend, and her whisper was low and urgent, making sure she wasn't overheard by the two men in the hall. 'You know I hate to blush,' she reproached him. 'I never did until I met you, and you make me worse by always remarking on it!'

'Only because I think it's delightful,' Manuel insisted, and bent quickly to kiss her mouth before the newcomers joined them.

Seeing them there was a surprise to both men, that was obvious, but José at least had no difficulty in reading the situation accurately and he paused in the doorway for a moment, blocking Esteban's way. He made a number of quick, smooth movements with his hands that Manuel seemed to have no difficulty understanding, because he was shaking his head.

'In fact Señorita Roderigo was making a start on breakfast,' he told José. 'Now that you've arrived you can take over; I'm quite sure the *señorita* will have no objection.'

José's small, sharp black eyes switched to her and their expression left no doubt that he knew exactly what had been going on. Esteban too made no secret of his interest and their almost casual acceptance of the situation gave rise to those discomfiting thoughts of other women again. Whether or not Manuel could face them with cool normality, Kristie couldn't, and she murmured an excuse before brushing past José in the doorway and walking quickly across the hall.

'Kristie!'

Both men followed his progress when he followed her from the room, and it was inevitable that speculation would be rife once the door had closed behind him, but just the same it was irresistible, when he called after her, to stop at the foot of the stairs. As she stood with one hand on the newel post Manuel placed his own long fingers over hers, pressing lightly while he looked into her face.

'*Now* they'll have something to gossip about,' she said, and laughed a little wildly.

'No one who works for me gossips about me,' Manuel assured her quietly. 'I have to trust them, Kristie, and I've never had cause to suspect I can't do so.'

'No, of course not.'

'Oh, Kristie!' He stroked a hand over her hair, then curved the same hand about her cheek, gazing at her with such a look in his eyes she felt she wanted to throw herself into his arms again, no matter who saw them. 'You constantly surprise me,' he murmured. 'I would never have believed you shy enough to run away because José and Esteban arrived—not when you first came here. How much I've learned about you, eh, my pigeon?'

'I—I was embarrassed just for a moment.'

It was true, yet Manuel seemed to suffer from no such reaction. He obviously felt no embarrassment at being caught in the kitchen with a young woman he had spent all weekend with alone, and in an obviously suspect situation, yet he seemed to understand her feelings. 'I know,' he said softly, and stroked his fingers down her neck. 'And I should say how sorry I am that I kissed you and made you blush, but——' he heaved his broad shoulders in a shrug, 'how can I say I'm sorry for something I enjoyed so much, eh?'

'You don't have to!' She spoke up quickly and it was impossible not to sound suspiciously breathless. Those caressing fingers on her neck aroused her as much as the look in his eyes did; mocking, teasing but hot with desire. 'I dare say they'll invent something much more lurid than what actually happened!'

'And you don't mind?'

'Of course I *mind*,' Kristie said, 'but it won't stop them speculating whether I mind or not, and I did bring this on myself by hiding away when I should have gone home.'

'Are you sorry you didn't go home, Kristie?'

The softness of his voice slid along her spine and she shuddered deliciously. 'No,' she declared, 'I'm not sorry.'

Manuel smiled as if it was exactly the answer he expected, then he leaned and kissed her mouth. 'Then let's go and wait in the *salón* while José prepares breakfast for us,' he suggested, but Kristie was shaking her head.

She needed a few minutes alone, a few minutes in which to decide what she was to say and do if Manuel decided to send her back to Seville with Esteban. If she pleaded to stay with him she couldn't be sure he would let her and he could be pretty adamant even in this more amenable mood. Also if she stayed she would only fall more and more deeply in love with him, and she still wasn't sure that that was likely to make for her happiness.

'I—I have something I want to do in my room,' she told him, and he shrugged resignedly.

Leaning down, he again brushed her lips with his. 'Then hurry, and come and have breakfast with me when you're ready,' he murmured.

Because she had a better idea now of how long breakfast took to prepare, Kristie wasn't very long, but as she came downstairs again she was startled to hear angry voices coming from the *salón*, men's voices which suggested than Manuel was quarrelling with Esteban, and she found that very hard to believe.

She hesitated at the foot of the stairs, not quite sure what she ought to do, and it had just occurred to her that the voice arguing with Manuel was alarmingly familiar, when the *salón* door burst open and Manuel came striding out with a frown as black as thunder on his face and his eyes glittering with furious anger.

She stared at him and her heart started a wild, urgent beat that filled her head, making her cling to the newel post. Seeing her, he came to a brief stop, then veered across in her direction and stopped immediately in front of her. There was no warmth about him now, only a fierce blazing anger that included her in its fury, and while she clung to the balustrade, staring at him dazedly, she caught her breath.

She saw him first from the corner of her eye and she could scarcely believe it was Juan who came, following

Manuel from the *salón* and looking incredibly wild-eyed and flushed. She supposed it was automatic when she stepped down another tread, but Manuel's harsh, abrupt instruction stopped her dead.

'Don't bother to come any further,' he told her roughly. 'Go back to your room and collect your things, Señorita Roderigo—you're going with your—cousin! The masquerade is over, but you were cleverer than I thought!'

Dazed and having no idea what had happened between them, Kristie put a hand on his arm, an automatic gesture that was meant to appease him but did nothing of the kind. 'Manuel——'

'Don't argue, get your things and go!'

'What's happened to make you——'

'Just do as I say, he's waiting!'

He turned and went striding off towards the room they had used as an office, leaving Kristie staring after him in blank bewilderment until he closed the door firmly behind him. Then she turned and looked at Juan, who stood in the middle of the hall, breathing hard and obviously keeping a firm hold on his temper.

'Juan——' She moistened her lips before she went on, and recognised the beginning of anger stirring in her as she put her own construction on the incident. 'Juan, what on earth are you doing here? How did you find me?'

It wasn't the way he expected her to react to his sudden appearance, that was obvious, and he watched her come across the hall towards him with a dark, defiant look in his eyes. 'I recognised the car your Señora de Mena came in,' he told her, 'and I followed it. I couldn't be sure it was coming here, but I was so desperate I'd have done anything.' He gripped her hands tightly and Kristie could feel the way he was shaking. 'Do as he said, my lovely, and get your things, I'm taking you home. I'd have come for you before if I'd known where to come; that—that seducer should be locked up for keeping you here!'

'He didn't keep me here!' Kristie's voice had a thick, shaky sound and she wasn't looking at Juan but at the closed door of the *salón*. 'I can't just go without——'

'He won't see you, Kristie,' Juan warned her. 'He knows exactly where he stands now and he won't give you any more trouble. Go on, darling, fetch your things and let's go, Mama's as anxious as I am now she knows the truth.'

'How could you tell her the truth when you don't know it yourself?' Kristie wailed despairingly. 'What did you say to Manuel to make him so angry? Tell me?' She didn't seriously expect him to answer, but she was serious about seeing Manuel before she left, if there was no alternative to her leaving, and she started across towards the office followed by Juan's anxious plea:

'Please, Kristie, let's go!'

It was Esteban who emerged from the office, as she approached, and his quick closing of the door behind him prevented her from getting even a glimpse of Manuel. 'I am sorry, *señorita*,' he told her, and Kristie had to believe he meant it, 'but the *señor* forbids me to let you in there. You're to pack and leave with—this gentleman.'

'But I *must* see him and explain!'

'I'm sorry, *señorita*. I'm to tell you to fetch your baggage and leave.'

It was like coming up against a brick wall, Kristie thought despairingly, and if Manuel had made up his mind that he wasn't going to see her again, she'd do better to accept the fact. To retain what little of her pride remained she should leave with Juan, but she would be leaving her heart with Manuel, and she no longer made any pretence of doing other than love him desperately.

With her head bowed she accepted defeat and without even looking at Juan again she went back upstairs to pack her bag. Juan had been responsible for Manuel sending her away so abruptly, and she would find it hard to forgive him, however well-intentioned he had been. She was so numbly unhappy that she didn't know what to say or do, but she would make him tell her what he had said to make Manuel so violently angry. Later when she had had time to recover a little, for at the moment she felt she would burst into tears if she even tried to speak.

Driving home in Juan's little car neither of them had said very much, although once or twice Juan had looked as if he was about to say something, then seemingly changed him mind. Aunt Maria had been tactful, welcoming her home but not asking too many questions, and for that Kristie had been grateful. Aunt Maria, she thought, saw a great deal more than her son did but was wise enough to keep her opinions to herself unless they were asked for.

It was later, when they sat together on the *patio*, that Kristie brought herself to the point of asking Juan exactly what had happened, and she had deliberately waited until the two of them were alone. 'I want to know exactly what happened,' she told him, fixing him with her darkly unhappy eyes. 'I know Manuel can be unreasonable at times, but I can't imagine what you told him that made him change so suddenly and so—so completely. What did you say to him, Juan?'

His lower lip was pursed slightly, and clearly he wasn't very keen on telling her, for he looked down at his hands rather than at her and Kristie took that as a bad sign. 'I simply told him what any man would have told him in my position.'

'In your position?'

Juan evaded her eyes still and he shrugged uneasily before he answered. 'I told him I objected to him keeping you there all weekend——'

'But he didn't keep me there. I hid myself in one of the turret rooms when the car came so that I wouldn't have to go back with it as he said I should.'

'Holy Mother!' Juan breathed piously, and stared at her in stunned disbelief. 'I can't believe it!'

'Nevertheless it's true. And Manuel stayed because he isn't the kind of man to leave a girl alone in an empty castle all weekend, and he sent José and Esteban home because they have families to see.'

He had noticed her use of Manuel's first name on several occasions and frowned over it, now he questioned it. 'Manuel?' he queried, and Kristie shook her head impatiently; in truth she was much closer to tears than she cared to admit.

'It's his name,' she said in a flat little voice, 'though I don't suppose I'll ever have the opportunity of using it again.'

'That matters?'

'It matters,' she admitted in the same expressionless voice. 'But go on, tell me what else you said.'

They were sitting either side of the little white *patio* table, and Juan traced a pattern on its top with a fore-finger, still keeping his eyes downcast. 'He said he'd writ-ten and explained the situation to your aunt and hoped she would understand. I told him that my mother might have been satisfied with his explanation, but my position was slightly different and I took a very different view of the situation.'

He raised his eyes briefly and looked at her, but when she eyed him suspiciously he hastily looked down again. 'Different?' she echoed, and Juan nodded.

It was clear that he would much rather not have gone on, but just as clearly Kristie wasn't going to be content with what little he had told her so far. 'I told him there was—an understanding between us,' he claimed, obvi-ously on the defensive, 'and that in the circumstances I took exception to you staying alone all weekend with another man and no one to chaperone you.'

Kristie almost moaned aloud and she closed her eyes for a moment in the agony of realisation, for she re-membered the number of times she had assured Manuel that there was nothing at all like that between her and Juan. Keeping a firm and determined hold on her temper, she put her hands over her face for a moment and tried not to blame Juan too much for what he had done.

'You have to admit there's some grounds for saying what I did,' Juan insisted anxiously. 'You know how I feel, Kristie.'

'I know how *I* feel,' Kristie told him, and her voice shook alarmingly despite her efforts to control it.

'Kristie, my pigeon!'

He reached for her hands, but Kristie drew them back, recalling too easily Manuel's long brown fingers clasping hers. 'And please don't call me that, Juan!'

He stared at her blankly for a moment, then his dark eyes narrowed slightly and showed some resentment. 'You used not to mind,' he said, watching her closely.

Kristie used her hands in a touchingly helpless gesture and shook her head. 'You may as well tell me the rest,' she said. 'And there has to be more, I know.'

'There's more,' Juan promised, this time with rather more relish, as if he had an inkling of what might have happened during that brief weekend and resented it. 'He didn't like being told that you weren't his for the taking and he looked as cold as ice when I let him know it. But he really blew his top when I added for good measure that it would make a marvellous story for the press.'

'Oh, Juan, no!'

'It got him right where it hurt most,' Juan went on relentlessly, his dark eyes gleaming. 'I asked him if he hadn't stopped to consider, before he got you there, what a story it would make; Manuel Montevio, the Golden Spaniard, keeping a young girl prisoner in his castle with no one else there but the two of them. I suggested it was quite a scoop, and one any reporter would give his—or her—right arm for, and for a minute I thought he was going to kill me.' He looked for a moment as if he still couldn't quite believe what he had seen, but Kristie could well imagine Manuel's reaction to a statement like that. 'Holy Mother,' Juan swore softly, 'I still believe he'd have killed me if that chauffeur hadn't knocked on the door and looked in for a moment.'

Kristie sat with her hands pressed close to her mouth and there was nothing more she could do to prevent the tears rolling slowly down her cheeks while she stared in blank hopelessness at the table-top. 'Oh, dear God,' she whispered. 'Juan, I'll never forgive you, never!'

'Kristie.' He was disturbed rather than angry now, and he tried to take her hands again, but again she snatched them back and pressed them once more to her mouth.

'Kristie, what did I do that was so awful? I know he doesn't like the press, he's hidden from reporters for years, including you, and it was just the worst thing I could think to wish on him.'

'But *I'm* a journalist,' Kristie reminded him in an anguished voice. 'Don't you think Manuel will think that's just what *I* intend to do? He probably thinks you were in cahoots with me to trap him into something like that. Don't you see? He probably thinks I planned it like this all along? He probably thinks that's why I hid myself away, to—to trap him.'

Juan was looking at her curiously, and his dark eyes were unhappy. 'Didn't you?' he asked quietly, and she closed her eyes and shook her head slowly, the tears still streaming down her face.

'No,' she whispered. 'I planned to—to make him tell me why he left motor-racing, but I didn't plan to—to humiliate him.'

'Or to fall in love with him?' Juan asked softly, and she immediately felt a curl of warning in her stomach. When she didn't answer him, Juan laughed shortly and shook his head. 'Oh, I know the symptons, my pigeon; who better?'

For a moment or two Kristie couldn't find the right words and she sat with her hands clasped tightly together and her eyes downcast. She had so often pushed the idea to the back of her mind of Juan feeling any more for her than a cousinly kind of love. Even just a moment ago when he had spoken of it she had preferred to think of it as merely a gesture of bravado, and she had been too involved in her own emotions to give much thought to Juan's. Now, realising that he really did love her made her feel oddly guilty in some way.

'Juan—I didn't know.'

She allowed him to take her hands and he held them tightly while he gazed at her with those dark expressive eyes of his. 'Oh, Kristie, my lovely, how could you *not* have known?' he asked. 'Haven't I made it obvious every time I'm near you? I love you, my pretty cousin, and I had hoped—at one time I' had hoped you felt something for me too.'

'Oh, Juan!'

She had never in her life before found herself in such a situation, and she felt horribly vulnerable, particularly as her emotions were still bruised from the last encounter with Manuel. She hated having to hurt Juan, but there was nothing she could do but let him know the truth, for she knew she would never be able to love anyone but Manuel.

'I'm sorry,' she whispered, and the tears again streamed down her cheeks. 'I'm so sorry, Juan.'

'So am I, my pigeon!' His smile had a hint of its old mischief, but his eyes were more gentle than she had ever seen them. He squeezed her fingers lightly, then raised them to his lips. 'For both of us.'

'He'll never forgive me,' Kristie whispered, returning to her own hurt, and Juan shook the hands he held as if in reprimand.

'How can he not?' he demanded. 'Unless he's made of ice, which I can't believe of any Spaniard with a temper like Montevio's, he'll find you too hard to forget to let you go right out of his life.' Again he pressed his lips to her fingers and the look in his eyes came too close to her heart for her comfort. 'I know I never could, my pigeon.'

CHAPTER NINE

KRISTIE had never felt so unhappy in her life before, and worst of all was feeling so helpless to do anything about it. Juan was much quieter than normal too, and she missed being able to confide in him, but it just wasn't possible, knowing how he felt about her. One way and the other she faced the fact that nothing could ever be the same again, and the only really logical thing for her to do would be to end her protacted holiday and go home.

Of course it would mean confessing to her editor that the whole thing had been a waste of time and that she wasn't going to produce the headline story she had promised. But that didn't concern her nearly so much as having to give up and go home without Manuel knowing the truth about that ridiculous threat of Juan's. It was *all* that concerned her at the moment.

What first put the idea into her head of going to see Señora de Mena and asking for her help, she had no idea, but she recalled how gentle and friendly-seeming Manuel's mother had been on both occasions when she met her. She couldn't even be sure that the *señora* would see her, but as far as Kristie could see she was her only hope of contacting Manuel and getting her side of the story across to him, and she was ready to try anything. A whole week had gone by since Manuel had so peremptorily ordered her from the castle, and she felt that she either had to do something positive or give up and go home.

It had seemed the natural thing to do to ask Juan for the loan of his car, or so she thought, but judging by Juan's reaction when she approached him it was the last thing he expected her to do. 'Certainly not!' he declared unhesitatingly. 'Are you quite mad?'

'Very likely!' The quick angling of her chin was instinctively defensive. 'But I have to do something, Juan, I can't just go on—sitting around like this.'

'Moping?' Juan suggested, with more of his customary mildness. He took her hands and held them tightly for a moment while he looked at her with such a depth of understanding in his eyes that it was almost her undoing. 'Oh, Kristie, my sweet darling girl, why? You know you're never going to get through to that arrogant, black-hearted devil; you've tried.'

'And I've succeeded,' Kristie insisted in a small, choked voice. 'Juan, if I could just let him know that that stupid threat you made was just sheer bravado, I know he'd understand. Señora de Mena is a nice, friendly woman and I'm almost certain she'll listen to me and tell Manuel the truth. I have to try, Juan.'

But Juan's mouth had a firm, stubborn look that she knew too well to suppose he was going to change his mind, and he squeezed her fingers gently while he shook his head. 'And get hurt all over again,' he prophesied. 'For your own good I can't let you do it, Kristie. I hate to see you looking as you have this past week, and whatever you feel for him, I can't forgive him for making you look like that.'

'You don't understand him.' She spoke in a small, hopeless voice that Juan found almost unbearably touching, and her mouth trembled as she sought to persuade him. 'If I can speak to Señora de Mena I know she'll do what she can——'

'You don't *know*, you only *hope*,' Juan interrupted quietly. 'No, I'm sorry, my lovely, but I won't be a party to anything that's likely to get you hurt even more than you are already.'

'You definitely won't let me have the car?'

'Not for this particular purpose—no, I'm sorry.'

Desperation made her angry and she drew back her hands, tightening them into fists as she looked at him, trying to keep back the tears that recently seemed to appear all too easily and too often. 'Then I'll have to find some other way,' she told him, and her voice was not quite as firm as she had hoped. 'I hoped you'd help me as you've always done, but obviously you've made up your mind, so I'll do it some other way.'

'You hoped I'd help you into the arms of another man?' Juan asked in a voice that shivered with emotion. 'You never did know *me*, did you, my lovely?'

The tears were a reality now, and she reached out to touch his hand lightly, apologetically, trying to measure his anguish against her own. 'I'm sorry, Juan,' she whispered.

'Oh, Kristie!' He seized her hands and pressed his lips to them, and his eyes were dark and earnest. 'Please don't go! You'll get hurt, and I can't bear to see you hurt any more.'

Kristie eased her hands away gently, tears shimmering in her eyes as she looked at him. 'I can't hurt any more,' she whispered, 'that's why I have to go, to try and put this right, don't you see?'

Juan gave up. He shrugged his shoulders in a slow, resigned gesture that said it all, and he shook his head. 'Yes, I see,' he said.

It seemed like a lifetime ago that Kristie had driven along this same road to the Villa de los Naranjos, as a passenger in a small grocery delivery van, determined to storm Manuel Montevio in his citadel. Now she was on her way there again and on more or less the same errand, except that it was an intermediary in the person of his mother whom she sought on this occasion.

How differently she had felt then too. Then she had been filled with excitement and some small anxiety in case her plan didn't work, pretty confident on the whole that she would get what she wanted. Crudely disguised as a boy because she didn't bother too much what impression she made. This time it was quite different, and she was half aware of the taxi-driver glancing at her every so often in the rear-view mirror as they took the San Pedro road out of Seville, curious about her pale face and heavy-rimmed eyes and the anxious way she bit into her lower lip.

The big iron gate was closed and padlocked as she remembered it, and the driver looked at her curiously when she asked to be let out, for it looked just as unwelcoming as ever it had done. 'You sure you've got the right place, *señorita*?' he asked, and Kristie nodded as she got out and paid him.

'Yes, I'm quite sure, thank you.'

He shrugged. 'Don't look as if you're expected,' he observed, taking note of the padlocked gate, and Kristie shook her head, not looking at him for fear he should realise how nervous she was.

'I'm not,' she told him in a small husky voice, 'but someone will come in a minute.'

The driver shrugged again, thrusting the fare into a pocket before he turned his vehicle around. 'If you say so,' he said.

Standing in front of the gate after he'd gone, Kristie wondered if in fact anyone would come in this instance. Then she remembered that Juan had gripped the gate and shaken it, and she did the same simply because she didn't know what else to do; afterwards peering anxiously through into the huge *patio* gardens.

It was almost like history repeating itself when the same elderly man came slowly around the bend in the path and eyed her suspiciously without making any attempt to open the gate. Kristie had never felt more alone or more vulnerable as she looked at him between the bars, and her voice had a shaky sound that betrayed just how she was feeling.

'I'd like to see Señora de Mena, please,' she said.

The old man's eyes took stock of her from below their wrinkled lids, and it was clear he wasn't going to admit her on demand. 'Is the *señora* expecting you, *señorita*?' he enquired politely, and Kristie's fingers tightened noticeably.

'No,' she admitted, 'but if you tell her that Kristie Roderigo is asking for her, I'm sure she'll see me. Please tell her I'm here.'

'Very well, *señorita*.'

He didn't sound as if he held out much hope and for the first time it occurred to Kristie to wonder what she would do if Señora de Mena would not see her. She was a long way from home, and she knew just how discomfiting the walk back to Seville could be; in her present state of mind she didn't think she could cope with it as she had on the last occasion.

'*Señorita.*' The man was back, turning a key in the padlock and swinging the gate wide to admit her, and Kristie's legs felt as if they were in danger of collapsing under her as she walked through. 'If you will follow me, *señorita.*'

It seemed so startlingly familiar, Kristie thought, and yet she had been there only twice before, and neither time via the main gate. The villa was every bit as impressive inside as out, and the coolness of a tiled floor and plain white walls came as a blessed relief after standing outside in the hot sun.

'Señorita Roderigo.' A cool hand clasped hers firmly, and Kristie found herself relaxing a little for the first time in days. Señora de Mena was too nice a woman to refuse her, she felt sure of it now that she had seen her again. 'Please come in, *señorita.*'

A huge cool *salón* overlooked the exquisite gardens that Manuel had told her his stepfather had planned and created, and there was such an air of tranquillity about the whole place that Kristie wondered how a character as wildly emotional as Manuel's could exist there. 'I don't— I'm not sure that you'll want to talk to me when you know why I've come, Señora de Mena.' Looking round anxiously she moistened her lips with the tip of her tongue. 'Manuel——'

'Is working up in the mountains, *señorita,*' she was assured, and Kristie heaved an inward sigh of relief. Only a moment ago it had occurred to her that Manuel might be home instead of working and she clasped her hands tightly together as she took a seat next to her hostess. 'You want to talk about Manuel?' Señora de Mena enquired softly.

'I—I wanted to ask you to help me tell him the truth, Señora de Mena.' She couldn't doubt that Manuel had told his mother at least some of what had happened at Castillo Cuchicheo, so she saw no point in beating about the bush. She had sworn to herself that she wouldn't cry, but there seemed nothing she could do about the tears that trembled on her lashes and partially hid her sight of the gently understanding features of the woman beside her. 'I must—explain, *señora*. Juan, my cousin, said things to Manuel that simply weren't true, but—but Manuel believed them and—and he wouldn't listen to me when I tried to speak to him. I have to make him understand how wrong he was.'

'And you hoped to persuade me to intercede with Manuel for you?'

The tone of her voice suggested that her cause was already lost, and yet Kristie couldn't give up yet. 'I don't know who else to ask for help,' she said. 'I have to get someone he'll listen to to make him understand, *señora*.'

The older woman's warm brown eyes were gentle with understanding. 'It must be very important to you,' she suggested, and Kristie in her anguish made no attempt to deny it.

'It is—very important,' she said.

'Ah!' Once more the dark eyes were looking at her and it was very difficult to guess exactly what was going on behind them. Then she shook her head slowly. 'But in that case you can do no better than explain to him yourself, my dear *señorita*.'

'But he wouldn't listen to me!'

'You say that without really knowing whether it's true or not,' Señora de Mena reproved her gently, but Kristie was convinced.

'I know Manuel,' she whispered, and did not for the moment realise to whom she said it.

'Allow me to know him just a little better, my dear.' She had been firmly but gently put in her place, Kristie realised, and bit her lip anxiously when the older woman got to her feet and pressed a call-button by the window.

'There is only one way to find out, I suggest,' Señora de Mena said, and her meaning was unmistakable, Kristie thought.

'You—you won't see him for me?' she asked, and the *señora* shook her head.

'I wouldn't be nearly such an effective advocate in your cause as you will be yourself, my dear, I promise you.'

Bitterly disappointed and feeling more wretched than ever, Kristie got to her feet. She had expected more of the *señora*, and yet she should have guessed that even his mother would probably think twice about tackling Manuel on a matter he felt so strongly about, and was so firmly convinced about. But at least she could make sure that she didn't have to walk back to Seville, and she tried to put on an appearance of normality as she made the request.

'I—I wonder if I might ask you to ring for a taxi for me, Señora de Mena. It's rather too far to walk back and I couldn't ask the man to wait.'

'That won't be necessary,' Señora de Mena told her quietly. 'I've rung for Esteban and he will take you up to Castillo Cuchicheo and leave you there.'

Kristie stared at her. 'But, *señora*——'

'Desperate measures, my dear child,' the older woman told her with a hint of a smile in her brown eyes. 'The castle is more than thirty kilometres up in the Sierra Morena and my son can do no other than take you in in the circumstances. A great deal can happen in four days, hmm?'

However much of a chance it was to take, Kristie couldn't resist it, but she remembered the last time she had been unexpectedly detained up there, and how much less trusting her aunt and Juan would be on this occasion. 'But I haven't any change of clothes, *señora*, and my aunt doesn't even know I've come here to see you.'

'Then I shall go and see her and explain,' the *señora* promised. 'As for your things—it will be a little inconvenient for you, I can see, but not impossible just for— shall we say twenty-four hours? If you can't persuade my son within twenty-four hours then I don't think you ever will, my dear, but I am confident that you will and I shall work on that assumption. Esteban will drive up there again tomorrow bringing some things for you; depending on what he finds he will either leave your suitcase or bring you back, do you agree?'

Kristie nodded, too bewildered with the speed of things to know what to say. She wished she shared the *señora*'s confidence that Manuel could be persuaded, but her heart was already rapping urgently at the thought of seeing him again, and she moistened her lips anxiously. How Juan would react to this latest situation, she dared not even think, but she prayed he wouldn't show up again at the Castillo Cuchicheo.

It was such an incredible feeling she had as they turned the last corner and the Castillo Cuchicheo came into sight that Kristie swallowed hard. Its walls rising from the depths of the chasm and its pointed turrets reaching for the sky, it still reminded her of a fairy-tale castle, and she felt another lump in her throat.

Catching her eye via the rear-view mirror, Esteban gave her an encouraging smile, as if he guessed how she must be feeling. 'My orders are to let you off by the drawbridge, *señorita*,' he told her. 'You'll be all right, you can't get lost, can you?'

'I hope not!'

Kristie laughed a little wildly as he braked the car to a stop and got out to open the door for her. How much he knew about her situation she had no idea, but he again smiled at her encouragingly. 'Good luck, *señorita!*'

Kristie smiled her thanks, but her heart was thudding almost painfully hard as she walked in through the arched gateway, plunged into its chill shadows for a moment, and her legs felt alarmingly weak. She turned and gave Esteban a wave just before he disappeared from her sight, but it was a gesture designed to boost her own morale as much as anything.

As she crossed the courtyard she noticed that some

remnants of her precious garden still decorated the rim of the fountain, obviously managing to survive in the water remaining in the basin, for the jet was no longer playing. Manuel had gone to so much effort to please her that she found it hard to believe he wouldn't at least listen to her when she tried to tell him how wrong Juan had been. That was how she consoled herself as she approached the huge outer door.

The door was closed as it mostly was and she hesitated for a moment, in doubt whether to knock and wait for admission, or whether simply to walk in. In the event the decision was taken from her when the door swung open and José stood looking at her, surprised at first and then with an unmistakable gleam of welcome in his small black eyes.

He invited her in with a sweep of his hand and led the way unhesitatingly across the hall to the little *salón* they had used as an office. He padded soft-footed just slightly ahead of her, while her own footsteps clicked briskly on the stone floor so that Manuel was almost bound to notice if he wasn't too deeply engrossed in his book.

It was just as if she was reliving that first time she had come to the castle when José opened the door and revealed Manuel standing with his back to the room, looking out of the window, and she caught her breath sharply, for the sight of him was so much more affecting even than she anticipated. Where he stood the sun caught his hair and turned it to a gleaming, burnished gold, and he had his hands clasped behind him; strong brown hands whose taut fingers betrayed the tension in him.

He turned in the same moment that José snicked the door shut, and his brows drew swiftly into a frown. 'Kristie! How on earth did you get back here?'

Kristie swallowed hard, for it wasn't exactly an encouraging opening and she could think only of throwing herself into his arms and being held close to that lean, earthy body while he kissed her. So fierce was her desire that she trembled like a leaf, and it became more important than ever to convince him he had misjudged her, because she could never live without him.

'Esteban brought me,' she said in a shiveringly small voice, and his frown deepened. 'He—now he's gone back.'

'Leaving you here?' She nodded. 'For how long?'

Again she swallowed hard before she answered. 'Twenty-four hours.'

'Ah!' He narrowed his eyes and tipped back his head and his gleaming amber eyes looked at her speculatively for a moment. 'You've been to see my mother,' he guessed, and it was much too difficult to tell whether or not he resented the fact.

So desperate was she for his understanding that Kristie believed she would have done anything, and Señora de Mena had been so confident that she would succeed. 'I— I went to see her to ask for her help,' she told him. 'I—I had to find some way of making you believe that what Juan told you wasn't true, and I thought Señora de Mena might—talk to you.'

'Instead of which she sent you to plead your own case?' he guessed, and a small, tight but not entirely humourless smile touched his mouth and offered the first sign of encouragement. 'Oh, the deviousness of women!'

'You wouldn't let me explain before I left here,' Kristie reminded him, 'and I had to do something to make you realise. I've just spent the most miserable week of my life trying to work something out and Señora de Mena seemed my only hope. I wasn't convinced, but she seemed to think I—I stood more chance of making you understand than she did, so she sent me up here and she's sending Esteban back tomorrow.'

'To fetch you back?'

His eyes hypnotised her and she moistened her lips with the tip of her tongue before she replied. 'He—he's bringing a suitcase with some of my things,' she told him, coming right out into the open. 'Either he'll leave the case or—take me back with him.'

'I see.' He moved his gaze slowly over her face and Kristie dared not look at him; she had too much at stake, and her heart was pounding mercilessly hard in her breast. 'The most miserable week of your life, you said. Did it matter so much to you, Kristie?'

His voice smoothed like a velvet glove along her spine, and she almost held her breath while the colour flooded into her face, something he was bound to notice as he always did. If only he would move nearer, or she dared move nearer to him, she would have felt there was more chance of his being ready to believe her.

'Tell me.' He still spoke softly, and she looked up to meet those curiously affecting eyes anxiously. 'What is it I have to understand, Kristie? Are you denying your cousin's claim to you? Or are you more concerned about the story he threatened to spread all over the newspapers? That *was* what brought you here in the first place, so why shouldn't I have believed it, Kristie?'

Holding her hands in front of her with the fingers clasped tightly together, she kept her eyes downcast. 'I know it's why I came here originally,' she admitted, 'but you must have a very bad opinion of me if you think——'

'And you can't deny that your cousin's in love with you,' Manuel interrupted softly.

Kristie couldn't deny it, however much she wished she could. 'But I'm not in love with him,' she insisted. 'And how could you believe I'd make news out of the weekend I had here with you? I can only think that—that your opinion of me is so low that you'll believe me capable of anything.'

'And you know that isn't true.'

He spoke softly and so gently that it was inevitable the ever-ready tears should fill her eyes again. 'I don't know anything of the sort,' she told him huskily. 'I only know that you ordered me out of your sight without giving me a chance to explain.'

'And then spent a week trying to convince myself that I could live with the thought of never seeing you again,' Manuel said quietly, and Kristie looked up swiftly, brushing the tears from her eyes so that she could see his face and judge his expression. 'It's true,' he said.

'Manuel——' She could get no further, for emotion choked her and made it impossible for her to say any more.

With his back to the window his face was mostly in shadow and his eyes half hidden by their thick lashes. The cream shirt he was wearing showed a slash of brown throat at the open neck and a shadow of dark flesh showed through its thin texture, while a pulse in his throat beat much more quickly than normal. Then he smiled and spread his arms wide and Kristie did not hesitate; she ran across the room and threw herself into his arms as she had been wanting to do ever since she came in.

He held her close, so close that his fierce virility took her breath away and she pressed her face against his chest, clasping her arms around him with her eyes closed in sheer ecstasy and her lips parted with the deep urgency of her breathing. Then he brushed a hand lightly over her silky black hair and touched his lips to her forehead, rocking slightly back and forth as he cradled her in his arms.

'Kristie, Kristie, my sweet adorable Kristie? How could I have ever let you go, my love?' His lips touched the soft skin of her neck as he nuzzled her ear and his voice was muffled by her hair. 'My mama is a devious woman,' he breathed, 'but she knows me better than I know myself, and I shall be eternally grateful to her for sending you back to me.'

Kristie felt she would have been content to stay exactly where she was for the rest of her life, but Manuel cupped his hands around her face and tipped back her head so that he looked down into her face. Long thumbs brushed lightly at the corners of her eyes and had the effect of making her look up at last.

Amber-gold eyes glowed with a promise of passion and she shivered. 'I love you,' Manuel said softly. 'If you hadn't come back to me, my pigeon, I'd have come for you, for I couldn't have faced the rest of my life without you. And if you'd refused me—I don't know what I would have done.'

'Did you think I ever *could* refuse you?' Kristie asked in a small shakey voice. 'Oh, Manuel, how little you know me!'

'So it would seem.' He brushed the hair back from her forehead with a light caressing hand while his eyes looked down at her in a way that could reduce any resistance she might have summoned to nothing. 'I shall make it my life's work to learn all there is to learn about you, my love.'

Lifting her arms, Kristie placed them around his neck and he put his hands in the small of her back and pressed her even closer. Her heart seemed long since to have stopped beating and the hard masculinity of him made her close her eyes as she lifted her mouth to be kissed. 'Manuel,' she whispered.

'I love you; Mother of God, but I didn't know anyone could love as much as I love you!' His mouth plunged downward, taking hers with the fierce, hard passion she had dreamed of all through the past days apart, and her body softened and yielded to the demands of his.

Sliding her hands into the back of his shirt, she pressed her palms to firm golden flesh, while his mouth buried itself in the softness of her shoulder. Big, gentle hands opened her dress while his mouth moved downward to the warm, pulsing softness of her throat and the pale scar on her breast.

When he eventually cradled her head in one hand and forced her to look up at him she met the boldness of glowing amber eyes with a smile of pleasure that left her feelings in no doubt at all. Her lips were parted and her cheeks flushed pink, and it was obviously too much for Manuel to resist when he remarked on it.

'You're blushing,' he whispered, and his voice still shivered with passion barely spent. 'I love it when you blush, my darling.'

Her pout of reproach lasted only a second or two, then she smiled up at him and her eyes were bright and shining with a kind of triumph. 'You're the only one who can make me blush,' she murmured, and the deep throatiness of his laughter shuddered through her body.

'I haven't even begun to make you blush, my own darling,' he whispered, and his eyes gleamed wickedly. 'Didn't you know that the Borgias were noted as much as lovers as they were as killers?'

'So?' Kristie challenged softly, and he kissed her hard.

'So,' he echoed, 'I hope you won't shrink from marrying one with Borgia blood in his veins, my lovely, because I mean to marry you and love you for the rest of our lives. I cannot put the reputation of the Borgias at risk.'

To Kristie nothing mattered but the fact that he wanted to marry her, and she would have taken him whatever his ancestry. Running her fingers through the thick red-gold hair above his ears, she smiled. 'I'd never shrink from marrying you, whoever you were,' she whispered. 'I love you.'

Just very briefly as he sought her mouth again Kristie recalled how determinedly she had pursued the Golden Spaniard for his story. Now she had no more need to pursue him, he was hers and she had never been more happy in her life, or cared less about her precious career.

 **ROMANCE**

Variety is the spice of romance

Each month, Mills & Boon publish new romances. New stories about people falling in love. A world of variety in romance – from the best writers in the romantic world. Choose from these titles in April.

NOT TO BE TRUSTED Jessica Ayre
THE OVERLORD Susanna Firth
WAIT FOR THE STORM Jayne Bauling
DAREDEVIL Rosemary Carter
THE SEA MASTER Sally Wentworth
BITTER REVENGE Lilian Peake
TROPICAL KNIGHT Lynsey Stevens
LONG COLD WINTER Penny Jordan
SHADOWED STRANGER Carole Mortimer
SMOKESCREEN Anne Mather
LOVE IS ETERNAL Yvonne Whittal
THE ICICLE HEART Jessica Steele

On sale where you buy paperbacks. If you require further information or have any difficulty obtaining them, write to: Mills & Boon Reader Service, PO Box 236, Thornton Road, Croydon, Surrey CR9 3RU, England.

Mills & Boon
the rose of romance

ROMANCE

Variety is the spice of romance

Each month, Mills & Boon publish new romances. New stories about people falling in love. A world of variety in romance – from the best writers in the romantic world. Choose from these titles in March.

STORMY VIGIL Elizabeth Graham
LAW OF THE JUNGLE Mary Wibberley
THE GOLDEN SPANIARD Rebecca Stratton
THE TRODDEN PATHS Jacqueline Gilbert
MAN OF TEAK Sue Peters
STAMP OF POSSESSION Sheila Strutt
LOVE'S DUEL Carole Mortimer
JUDITH Betty Neels
NOT FAR ENOUGH Margaret Pargeter
DISHONEST WOMAN Jessica Steele

On sale where you buy paperbacks. If you require further information or have any difficulty obtaining them, write to: Mills & Boon Reader Service, PO Box 236, Thornton Road, Croydon, Surrey CR9 3RU, England.

Mills & Boon
the rose of romance

Mills & Boon
Best Seller Romances

The very best of Mills & Boon Romances
brought back for those of you who missed
them when they were first published.
In March
we bring back the following four
great romantic titles.

DARK HILLS RISING
by Anne Hampson

When Andrew MacNeill married Gail he made it clear that he did
not want a wife but a mother for his children; Gail, having thought
marriage was not for her since she had been badly scarred and
injured in an accident, told herself that all she wanted was to have
some children – any children – to mother. But was either of them
being completely honest?

LOVE IN DISGUISE
by Rachel Lindsay

Because Mark Allen, a high-powered tycoon, preferred his
housekeeper to be an elderly woman Anthea assumed a disguise
to get the job. But no disguise could hide her awareness of her
acid-tongued employer or help to conceal her dislike of the lovely
Claudine, who seemed determined to marry Mark. Yet . .

HEART IN THE SUNLIGHT
by Lilian Peake

Norway, Noelle found when she went to work there, was a land of
sunlight, glorious scenery and charming people – with the exception,
unfortunately, of her boss, the infuriating Per Arneson!

DEAREST DEMON
by Violet Winspear

Destine felt that her life had ended when her young husband was
killed only hours after their wedding. In an effort to forget she took
a job in southern Spain – and met the man who, in all the world,
was the most likely to remind her of that tragedy she only wanted
to forget .

FREE
information leaflet about the Mills & Boon Reader Service

It's very easy to subscribe to the Mills & Boon Reader Service. As a regular reader, you can enjoy a whole range of special benefits. Bargain offers. Big cash savings. Your own free Reader Service newsletter, packed with knitting patterns, recipes, competitions and exclusive book offers.

We send you the very latest titles each month, postage and packing free – no hidden extra charges. There's absolutely no commitment – you receive books for only as long as you want.

We'll gladly send you details. Simply send the coupon – or drop us a line for details about the Mills & Boon Reader Service Subscription Scheme.
Post to: Mills & Boon Reader Service, P.O. Box 236, Thornton Road, Croydon, Surrey CR9 3RU, England.
*Please note – READERS IN SOUTH AFRICA please write to: Mills & Boon Reader Service of Southern Africa, Private Bag X3010, Randburg 2125, S. Africa.

Mills & Boon

FREE
Mills & Boon
Reader Service
Catalogue

The Mills & Boon Reader Service Catalogue lists all the romances that are currently in stock. So if there are any titles that you cannot obtain or have missed in the past, you can get the romances you want DELIVERED DIRECT to your home.

The Reader Service Catalogue is free. Send for it today and we'll send you your copy by return of post.

the rose of romance

Masquerade
Historical Romances

Intrigue excitement romance

THE GOLDEN BRIDE
by Ann Edgeworth

When Lalia Darrencourt, heiress and acknowledged Victorian beauty, is jilted by her fiancé a week before her wedding she is convinced she wants nothing more to do with love, but when she discovers her mistake it is almost too late . . .

PRINCE OF DECEPTION
by Valentina Luellen

On her arrival in St Petersburg, Emma Fraser is horrified to find that the man she took to be a fellow servant is Prince Michael, head of the House of Adashev. How can she trust him when he has already deceived her once – especially when he seems to be so closely involved with the Czarina Catherine.

Look out for these titles in your local paperback shop from 12th March 1982